Joe and Wishbone stopped before they entered the park.

It was so dark that it was impossible to see the path that Joe usually took.

"Gee, it's dark," Joe said uncertainly. "Too dark to bike, I think. And it's so quiet, it's a little bit creepy."

He took a tentative step forward. His sneakers crunched on the pebbly path.

Something rustled in the distance. Joe stopped. "Maybe this shortcut was a bad idea," Joe admitted.

Just then, a sound split the silent night.

"What was that?" Joe stopped so short that he bumped into Wishbone.

"Sounds like—" Wishbone said. Then he felt something prickling up along his fur. "Sounds as if it's coming closer . . ."

Other books in the
Adventures of **wishbone**™ series:

Be a Wolf!

Salty Dog

The Prince and the Pooch

Robinhound Crusoe

Hunchdog of Notre Dame

Digging Up the Past

The Mutt in the Iron Muzzle

Muttketeer!

A Tale of Two Sitters*

Moby Dog*

*coming soon

The Adventures of WISHBONE™

ROBINHOUND CRUSOE

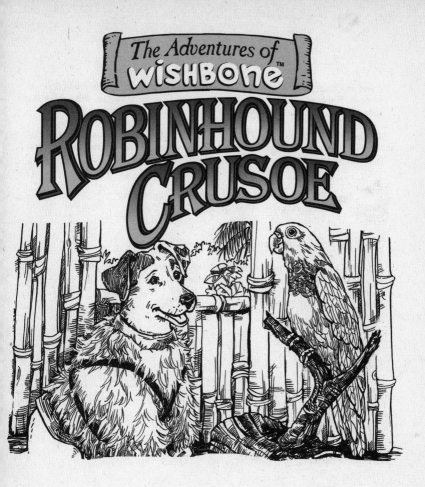

by Caroline Leavitt
Inspired by *Robinson Crusoe* by Daniel Defoe

WISHBONE™ created by Rick Duffield

Big Red Chair Books™, *A Division of **Lyrick** Publishing*™

This book is a work of fiction. The characters, incidents, and dialogues are products of the author's imagination and are not to be construed as real. Any resemblance to actual events or persons, living or dead, is entirely coincidental.

 Big Red Chair Books™, *A Division of Lyrick Publishing*™
300 E. Bethany Drive, Allen, Texas 75002

©1997 Big Feats! Entertainment

Edited by Kevin Ryan

Copy edited by Jonathon Brodman

Cover design by Lyle Miller

Interior illustrations by Jane McCreary

Cover concept by Kathryn Yingling

Wishbone photograph by Carol Kaelson

ISBN: 1-57064-271-0

First printing: August 1997

10 9 8 7 6 5 4 3 2

Printed in the United States of America

For Max,
who loves all dogs

FROM THE BIG RED CHAIR . . .

Oh . . . hi! Wishbone here. You caught me right in the middle of some of my favorite things—books. Let me welcome you to THE ADVENTURES OF WISHBONE. In each of these books I have adventures with my friends in Oakdale and imagine myself as a character in one of the greatest stories of all time. This adventure takes place during the same time period as the first season of my television show, when Joe and his friends are twelve and in sixth grade. In *ROBINHOUND CRUSOE*, I imagine I'm Robinson Crusoe, from the book *ROBINSON CRUSOE*, by Daniel Defoe. It's an exciting tale about a man who must live by his wits when he's shipwrecked on a deserted island for many years.

You're in for a real treat, so pull up a chair and a snack and enjoy *ROBINHOUND CRUSOE*!

Chapter One

It was Sunday afternoon at four-thirty in Oakdale, and Wishbone sat hopefully in a corner of the driveway while Joe practiced shooting his basketball into the hoop above the garage.

"Joe, you've been practicing since three," Wishbone said. "How about at least practicing something different? It's a perfect fall day. We could work on 'Let's take the dog for a walk.' Or how about 'tug-of-war'? I've got a sock in mind that's perfect for the job!"

Joe shot another basket.

"Joe, Joe," Wishbone called. "Practice makes perfect, but don't you think it's important to get some *team* spirit in here—team, as in you and I together? Not that I mind being cheerleader, since, after all, I'm your biggest fan. But give me a chance to play. I could surprise you. It could be *my* pet project."

Joe leaped up and shot another basket, landing the ball cleanly into the hoop. "The crowd cheers!" Joe shouted. "There's a new champ in town, and his name is Talbot!"

"And there's also a dog in town who needs

some attention—and his name is Wishbone!" said Wishbone.

The side door of the Talbot house opened and Ellen poked her head out. "Joe, you've been practicing for weeks. And today you've practiced more than enough! You're as ready for that game as you'll ever be. Why don't you relax a little?"

"Yes, come on, Joe," said Wishbone. "I'm just the dog to show you how it's done! We could take a walk, we could take a nap—that sort of thing."

Joe jumped up, making one more basket. "I know, I know, but this is my big chance. I could make a name for myself. I even get to be the point guard. Then I get to make the baskets and score. This isn't just any city league game we're playing tonight. It's totally different. Every team is made up of players from a bunch of different schools. There are only three people from my school on my team. It's kind of a match among different school districts. Mom, the eighth-grade coach is going to be there checking out new talent."

"Check out *this* talent," Wishbone said, then leaped high into the air. He turned in a back flip and landed perfectly on all fours.

Joe twirled the basketball on his fingertips. "I've got to do well. I just have to stand out so the coach sees me. This could be my big chance to make the team when I get to junior high school, Mom," Joe said.

Ellen gave a half-smile. "I thought the main idea of playing sports was to show cooperation, not just competition," she said. "Learning the elements of teamwork is very important."

Joe shook his head. "This could be the start of something really, really exceptional for me, Mom. You have to think big."

Wishbone's ears perked up. "Hey! That's my cue. Joe, how about a big walk? How about a big pat on my head? Or a big belly rub?"

Joe tucked the ball under his arm. "Well, I know I've perfected that new layup. And my jump shot is pretty good."

"Jump? You want to talk 'jump'?" Wishbone's ears perked up. He jumped as high as he could into the air again. "Talented *and* cute. How can you beat that combination?"

Ellen winced and placed one hand over her jaw. "Okay, Joe, I'm just going to see the dentist. This toothache is making me feel miserable."

Wishbone looked up. "Chew on the furniture, Ellen. That's the secret to keeping my pearly whites in shipshape condition. And I don't mind if I join you. Might I suggest the dining room chairs?"

Ellen glanced up at the sky. "I don't like the look of this weather, but I was lucky the dentist could see me on a Sunday, never mind at this late hour. I should be back in time to take you to the game." She jiggled her car keys in her hand. "I didn't have time to go shopping, so we can go out to eat to celebrate after the game." She ruffled Joe's hair affectionately.

"I know there will be something to celebrate," Joe said intently.

"Oh, Joe," Wishbone said, "why don't we kill two birds with one stone and take a walk now? That way, we'll have quality time together. If it rains, we can forget about that bath you were talking about giving me later."

"I had better get going. See you later." Ellen bent and scratched Wishbone behind his ears.

"Oh, that hit the spot," Wishbone said with a contented sigh.

Joe checked his watch. "I guess I should stop practicing," he said. "I don't want to wear myself out." He started to go inside the house. "Come on, Wishbone."

"You're stopping your practice? 'Atta boy, Joe!" Wishbone said.

Inside, without Ellen, Joe noticed how very quiet the house seemed to be. Joe and Wishbone climbed the stairs up to Joe's bedroom. Joe stood in the center of the room and flexed and unflexed his arm muscles. Wishbone wandered over to the stereo.

"Want to put some music on or something?" Wishbone asked. "Music to pet dogs by?"

Joe continued working out for what seemed forever, not paying any attention to Wishbone.

"I guess not," Wishbone said, resigned to being ignored.

Suddenly, from outside, there was a crack of thunder, followed by a flash of lightning. Wishbone felt his fur stand on end, and he scooted under the bed.

"Wow!" Joe said, startled. "That was close." He looked around. "Wishbone, where are you? Wishbone?" Getting up from his exercise mat, Joe scouted around for the dog. "Wishbone!" he called.

Wishbone's nose poked out from under the bed.

Joe crouched down and rubbed Wishbone's nose. "There's nothing to be afraid of. We're safe inside with all the comforts of home."

"Who's afraid?" said Wishbone indignantly, crawling out from under the bed. "I was just doing an inventory-control check, that's all. It's very important to keep checking your stock because you never know when you might need it. I wanted to see if that shoe I was chewing was still there."

There was another clap of thunder, and Wishbone jumped. He poked his nose under the bed again.

"Yup. There it is. The shoe. Still there. Big. Blue. Nicely chewed at the toe, but the heel still needs work. I'll have to get right on it," Wishbone said.

"Well, back to work," Joe said. He lifted his arms again, when there was a sudden boom of thunder and a flash of lightning. The lights in the house flickered off and on.

"What was that?" said Joe. "Oh, great, I hope it's not the power going out."

The phone rang. "Let it ring," Joe said. "We've got an answering machine." He studied himself in the mirror. "The name of the game is . . . basketball!" he said.

"The name of the dog is . . . Wishbone!" Wishbone said.

"Think of it," Joe said. "This could be just the start of something really big. People could begin to notice how good a player I am."

The phone rang again.

"I'd fetch the call if I were you. It could be important," Wishbone said, tilting his head as the answering machine clicked on.

Ellen's voice crackled over the line. "Hi, Joe, it's Mom. Listen—"

"Joe, it's Ellen," Wishbone said. "Even with my superior hearing, her voice sounds muffled. Ellen, speak louder. Belt it out as if you really mean it."

"Joe, honey," Ellen's voice said, "I hope you can hear me. I'm using someone's cellular phone. I'm going to be a little late. Something's wrong with the car's transmission. If you need me, I'm at—" The sound stopped and there was a hissing noise.

"Ellen?" said Wishbone.

"At where?" said Joe. "Maybe I should call the dentist." He picked up the phone and dialed. "Busy," he said, hanging up. Joe checked his watch. "And . . . and . . . we have to get going to the game." Just then the overhead light began to sputter and dim. "Oh, no, don't go out now!" Joe begged. Both he and Wishbone stared at the light fixture. There was a sizzling sound. Suddenly the room was plunged into darkness.

"Oh, great! Maybe it's just a blown fuse," Joe said.

"Come on, Wishbone, let's check the fuse box. I bet we can clear this up in no time."

Wishbone headed for the kitchen and then went toward the basement stairs. He sniffed the air. "This doesn't look like the same house, but at least it *smells* like the same house."

Joe squinted. "This is kind of spooky," he said. "The whole house seems so pitch-dark." He walked through the kitchen and opened the basement door. "It's even darker down there. I can't see a thing. I can't even see the basement stairs."

"Me, either," Wishbone said.

"I'd better get the flashlight," Joe said. "Let's see, Mom usually keeps it in the top drawer." He fished in the drawer by the stove. "No flashlight," Joe said. "Where else could it be?"

"Uh . . . Joe—" Wishbone said, turning back toward the living room and barking for Joe to follow him.

"Where are you going, Wishbone? I can hardly see you."

"Follow my voice," Wishbone said, and then he barked so Joe could follow his voice.

"Come on, we have to find a flashlight," Joe said.

Wishbone barked again, and then he tugged at Joe's pants leg.

"All right, what's so important?" Joe said, following Wishbone into the living room.

Wishbone bent down and put both front paws under the living room sofa. "It's the latest addition to my museum," Wishbone said, rolling out the flashlight and picking it up in his jaw. "All right, I admit it.

It's not part of the permanent collection. I got it on loan from Ellen, but I'm hoping she'll donate it."

"Great! The flashlight!" Joe said, switching it on. A thin beam of light illuminated a small patch of the floor in front of them. "This helps a little," he said. "Let's get to the basement."

Joe and Wishbone carefully made their way down the stairs and into the basement. They shone the flashlight in front of them, taking one cautious step at a time. The light cast strange, eerie shadows along the wall.

"Boy, it's creepy down here," Joe said.

Wishbone had to agree.

Joe put one hand on the wall for balance. "Let's see, the fuse box is on the left."

"I'm right beside you, Joe!" Wishbone said.

Joe stumbled against a box on the floor. "Ouch!" he said, rubbing his leg.

"This way, Joe." Wishbone barked.

"The fuse box," Joe said. "All I have to do is flip the switches on the circuit breakers." He opened the box and went to work. "Hey! What's going on here?" Joe said. "It's *still* pitch-dark in here." Joe sighed. "Let's head back upstairs."

"Wishbone, master guide, at your service!" Wishbone said, leading the way.

Upstairs, Joe shone the flashlight around the otherwise dark kitchen. Then he and Wishbone went toward the front of the house. "All the power is out," Joe said. He pointed the flashlight at the sofa.

Joe looked out the window. Wishbone jumped up next to him and looked outside, too. Usually at that time of day there were kids playing outside, or neighbors talking.

There was light. But now, outside it was completely dark and so empty. It seemed as if Oakdale had been completely transformed. Wishbone heard the sudden dull rumble of a car driving slowly by. The headlights threw thin beams of light across the living room wall. Then the room became completely dark again.

"Wait a minute here," Joe said. "*All* the lights in the entire neighborhood are out. All the electricity. I don't see a single person. It feels as if we're the only ones here in this entire neighborhood!"

"On the plus side, I'm *great* company," Wishbone said enthusiastically.

"It must be a blackout," Joe said. "We're on our own here, Wishbone. Stuck in darkness. The school I'm playing at is across town. Maybe there is no black-out there. I have to get to the game. I just have to." Joe shone the flashlight at his watch. "It's already almost five o'clock! How will I get there? What are we going to do, Wishbone?"

Oh, no! No lights, no Ellen with her car, and no electric can opener. It's the end of Joe's civilization as he knows it—and the end of my dinner! You know, it reminds me of another story, in which a man is pitted against the forces of nature. The tale is Daniel Defoe's rousing adventure story, *Robinson Crusoe*, written back in 1719. Robinson Crusoe was a young Englishman who battled the forces of nature with nothing but his wits—just as Joe and I are about to do!

Chapter Two

Wishbone sniffed an adventure coming on. He imagined that *he* was Crusoe, a stubborn young lad at home in England, yearning to go to sea.

You know, the only thing more exciting than an adventure story is a true-life adventure tale! To make his novel seem like a true story, Defoe wrote it like a *memoir,* which is a fancy name for a journal—kind of like the way *canine* is a fancy name for *dog!*

Wishbone could see it all now. He was Robinson Crusoe, writing down his tale for future generations to read and learn from. He was now very old, and his fur was white. His tail had a little less wag, his body less bounce to the ounce. But as he retold his story, he imagined he was growing younger and younger. His fur took on more shine, and he had more spring in his step. He was suddenly scampering back in time to 1659 in London, England, becoming the young lad Crusoe. He was standing on all fours in his father's richly appointed study, asking permission to seek his fame and fortune at sea. Pen in paw, Crusoe began to write his story:

I was as itchy to go off to sea as if the very fleas on my coat had doubled and there was not an ounce of flea powder in sight. I had seen an advertisement for a ship bound for Africa. The ad was asking for men to sail her. The ad read: COME TO THE DOCKS OF LIVERPOOL. SAILORS NEEDED. SOME NEED NOT BE EXPERIENCED. I knew the inexperienced men would be paid less in exchange for their training. But I was so excited, I tore down the sign with my teeth and stashed it in my coat pocket. I didn't have much time to get my parents' permission because the ship would be at port in less than a week.

My parents were good people. My father was a businessman who ran a hat shop. Nothing would have given him more pleasure than for me to help him run it. Already, I had seen the sign he had painted: CRUSOE & SON. It stood inside the shop, waiting for the day when he felt I was ready to be his partner. Every time my father saw it, he smiled. Every time I saw it, I felt myself go numb, from my nose to my tail. I didn't want that kind of life. I was too good for it. I was as proud as if I were Best of Show. I wanted something better—something much more exciting than a plain old job. I wanted adventure and danger and thrills!

I had never disobeyed my father before or questioned his plans for me. When he said I should go to school, I went. But now I stood before my father, tail held high, and pleaded my case.

"I'm young. I should be having adventures. Going off to sea could be the greatest fun of my life. I can always join the hat company later."

"Son," said my father, "please stay at home. Be content with what you have. London is a wonderful city to live in."

"Maybe for you," I answered, "but I'm young and healthy and in want of new roads to follow, new seas to sail, and new bones to bury! I want new ground to cover—and to dig in! I can't be satisfied just with making hats."

"Please listen to me," said my dear father. "Your mother and I love you deeply and want you safe at home. You'll be happy if you stay at home. Making hats is a good profession. You can feel proud making a beautiful hat."

"Not as proud as I'd feel sailing the high seas," I replied.

"If you go abroad, I fear you'll end up miserable." My father shook his head sadly. "I love you, son. I want you to be happy, and so I can't consent."

I could hear the sound of a chicken being roasted a mile and a half away, but I couldn't let myself hear this. I folded my ears over, refusing to listen. When I looked up, my father seemed so sad that I hung my tail between my legs.

"What ship did you plan to sail?" he finally asked.

I had never lied to my father before, but I knew if I told him, he would do his best to stop me. So I lied. "No particular ship," I said.

"You have never questioned my judgment like this before," my father said. "It makes me feel as though I am losing you. That causes me to feel very sad."

"You won't lose me," I said. *Only for as long as a sea voyage or two,* I thought, but I kept silent. I didn't wish to hurt him any more. But I couldn't help myself from still wanting to be on the docks when that ship was ready to sail.

Maybe my mother will say yes, I thought. I approached her next, practically sitting up and begging for her help.

"Can't you speak to Dad? He listens to you," I said. "Just let me go to sea, just this once. If it doesn't work out, I'll come home. I'll never mention the sea again—I won't even ask to go to the beach!"

Crusoe's mother sighed. "Son, the sea is cold and

damp. A ship is dangerous. At home you have all the food you could want, all the warm bedding. You can have a good job working with your father at the hat company. And, certainly, you can have all the love you desire."

"That isn't enough," I said. "Those are merely creature comforts. I need to feed my soul!" I looked on my mother with great love, but even as I stretched to kiss her cheek, I could hear the roar of the sea in my ears. It called out to me.

"Please forget this nonsense about sailing," my mother said to me.

No matter how I tried, I couldn't forget. The call of the sea, and all the wealth and fame, was as irresistible to me as having a frisky cat to chase. Almost immediately, I began packing my bags to set sail, hiding them deep in my closet so my parents wouldn't find them.

The day the ship was scheduled to set sail, I woke up two hours earlier than usual. My parents were still sleeping. I crept into their rooms. As I watched them sleep, my heart was filled with love and sadness. I knew how upset they would be by my departure, but the pull of the sea was too great. *This life might be fine for you, dear parents, but I need more,* I thought. I tiptoed to their bed and quietly kissed my father and mother, not wanting to awaken them. Then, tail wagging, I stepped out the front door and into a future filled, I hoped, with adventure and glory.

It was a fall day as crisp as a biscuit. It didn't take

me long to get to Liverpool and head for the docks.
The docks were broad brown wood, jutting out into
the ocean. There were lots of people milling
around—and, to my great excitement, lots of ships!
At least five of them were tied up at the docks. Each
ship was so large I had to crane my neck to take in
the view of an entire one. The ships had long inclin-
ing planks called gangplanks running from the deck
to the dock. Dockworkers were loading great boxes
into some ships, and out of other ships. Women were
kissing their men goodbye as the sailors climbed up
the gangplanks and vanished into the ships. Little
children were waving farewell. Everyone seemed to
have someone to see them off. For a moment, I
missed my father and mother so much that it made
my heart ache and my tail droop.

I approached each ship, asking whatever sailor I could find which ship was bound for Africa. I was getting more and more excited. There was always a man standing by the gangplank of each ship, ticking off the names of each person who boarded.

"Are you connected with the ship that put up the advertisement for sailors?" I asked. The first two men shook their heads no, ignoring me. The third man I asked, however, nodded his head yes. He looked me up and down, from my nose to my tail, then laughed.

"Inexperienced, am I right?" he asked.

"You are right, but not for long," I said.

"Climb aboard," he said. "Go talk to the captain."

"How will I know him?" I asked.

The man grinned. "You'll know who he is the first time you see him."

The boat was a tall sailing ship built of heavy, deep-brown wood. It was so large I had to stretch my neck back just to see the top of it. It had six large billowing white sails. It was big enough to carry sixteen men and 120 tons of cargo.

"Seems shipshape to me," I said, admiring the smooth deck and the sails. I couldn't believe it. My great dream was coming true. I was on board a ship, and I would be sailing soon. My heart beat so fast that I felt like chasing my tail around and around with absolute glee.

There was a tall, stern-looking man who wore a high hat. He was unfolding a map and frowning at it. This, I suddenly was sure, must be the captain.

"Hello!" I called to the captain. "I saw your ad for

sailors—especially inexperienced ones. Do you need any more sailors? I will do anything."

The captain studied me for a moment. "Come aboard, then. We'll try you out," he said.

Chapter Three

I had never been so happy! I was a sailor. I was on a ship. Since I was a new sailor, my duties were usually to wash down the decks and help out the other sailors. My first job, though, was to help raise and lower the sails so that they might catch the wind and move the ship forward. I pulled the ropes of the sails in my jaw, until the sails were high above us, catching the wind as easily as I caught a ball.

The wind ruffled the fur along my back most pleasurably. I perked up my ears and my whiskers.

The crew soon sailed toward the African coast. Unused to the sea, I began to feel queasy. The deck rocked and rolled. I spent most of my time hanging onto the railing for dear life. *All I need to do is to get my sea legs working,* I thought—*all four of them.*

The crew laughed and mocked me. "You look seasick!" the captain called. He shook his head at me in disapproval. "Being a sailor is my calling, but for you, it seems a kind of test. What are you trying to prove—and why?"

Hesitantly, I told him about my father's wish for

me to stay at home, and how I knew that was not the way of life for me. "I knew I could go to sea and distinguish myself by having adventures," I said.

The captain shook his head gravely. "Adventures! Why did I ever take you on board my ship? You're wet behind the ears. Go back to your father and stop tempting fate. If you don't go back, you will meet with nothing but disaster!"

I didn't listen. The ship continued to sail, and I stayed on board. We sailed for a few months.

All was fine until we had reached the southern tip of Italy. Then the skies suddenly darkened with clouds, blotting out all sunlight. A chill bit deep into my bones and fur, and I curled up as tightly as I could for warmth. I tucked my tail between my legs. Then I used my paws to cover my nearly frozen face. Almost immediately, a storm erupted, unleashing great torrents of rain and hail. The storm brought winds that seemed to tear right into the very heart of the ship.

"Batten down the hatches!" cried the captain.

"Never mind the hatches! Batten down me!" I yelped, digging my paws into the deck as if I could fasten myself there with my nails.

The wind began to whip at the ship, faster and harder. Finally, one of the great sails ripped in two with a great tearing noise. This made the ship sway to and fro, and I became even more seasick.

"Get belowdecks!" the captain cried out to me. "See if there is any flooding!"

I pulled at the door with teeth and paws, but the force of the wind yanked me away.

The sea water began flooding onto the decks. It

drove sailors to their knees. The force of the water and the size of the waves washed one man nearly overboard. "Help!" he cried, clinging to the ship's edge.

I trotted over and grabbed his hand with my paws, holding him as tightly as I could. I tried my best to pull him back onto the ship. Just then a great swirling wave washed over both of us. It must have been ten feet high.

"Hold on tight!" I cried out to the sailor.

"I can't!" he replied. He let go. To my absolute horror, he was flung into the foamy, wild sea.

"Man overboard!" I yelled. My voice was lost in the violent roar of the ocean. When I looked back into the water for the sailor, he was gone—vanished. All remaining crew members were gripping onto the railings for their own dear lives.

"Get to the pump room!" the captain cried. "It's flooding with water."

Instantly, six sailors struggled to get belowdecks. I tried to follow, but I fell on the slippery deck, and I was flung against the railing. I held on as hard as I could, trying to stand.

Every time I saw a great wave approach and then crash down on the ship, I was sure my life would end. My fur was so wet I felt as if I were wearing a soaked towel. I couldn't see because the rain and sea water kept beating against my face.

"I vow that if I ever get out of this mess, I will go directly home to my father and mother and never set any of my four paws on the sea again!" I cried.

The storm continued to rage in all its fury, well into the night, making my whiskers stand on end. . . .

Then, just as suddenly as the storm had come upon us, it ended.

The air cleared. The rain stopped. The ship suddenly began to sail more smoothly again. I loosened my grip on the railings. The sea had calmed, and the sun shone a beautiful golden light upon the water. It was like the butter I liked to lick. Better than that, we were near the shore. The captain told us to take the day off at port.

"Boy, that was a scare! I think my sailing days are over," I told the captain.

"Yes," he said gently. "I know I asked for inexperienced men, but you are a bit too green. It is the best thing for both of us." He wished me good luck, and I hurried off to shore.

Some of the seamen and I soon went into a cozy tavern. There I sat myself down by the fire and had a fine meal of steak and bones, licking both the plate and my chops clean. Soon all my fears vanished. Any kind of water seemed fine and safe to me, even the water of a bath, which surely was not my favorite thing in the world.

"Let's make a toast to our good fortune," one of the other seamen said.

I licked at the rim of my glass.

"That was no storm," said another. "That was just a little cupful of wind!"

Soon I forgot my promise and all my fears of being swallowed up by the sea. The very next day—

September 1, 1659—I found another ship, this one bound for China, and I signed on as a sailor. "This time I'm experienced and know what I'm doing," I said. "Fear is not my middle name. It's Michael."

This China-bound ship, while not as large as the last one I sailed, seemed very seaworthy. It had four big sails and a smooth, long deck and carried forty men. I felt even safer to note that this ship carried four sturdy-looking lifeboats. Each lifeboat was slung along the side of the ship by heavy ropes.

This time, everything went smoothly on the ship for nearly three weeks. Then a storm began, and it raged so terribly that even the most seasoned of the seamen grew white with fear. The waves were so high and so fierce that they ripped through two of the main-sails. I climbed the mast with two other sailors to try to secure one of the sails. The storm tossed the ship so that it seemed to lose its balance. It began to tilt. I hung onto the ropes of the mast by my paws and teeth. For the first time in my life, I wished for a leash, so that it could hold me safely to the ship!

A huge wave splashed over me, soaking my fur and pulling the ship nearly onto its side. Terrified, I whined deep in my throat as the ship trembled and nearly turned almost completely on its side. Suddenly, the wind screamed toward us from the other direction. It hit us with such force that the ship was flung right-side up again. I was thrown down from the mast and onto the deck. I scrambled for the railing, fighting to hold on.

"The storm is throwing us off course!" the first mate called, grabbing the ship's big wheel. "I don't know where we are."

He struggled to put the ship back on course. The storm rocked the ship so violently that he was thrown from the wheel onto the deck. I climbed up on the mast to try to unfurl some of the sails to slow down the ship. I got as far as halfway when the wind became so fierce that it was all I could do to cling by my paws.

"I've never seen the weather so treacherous!" a sailor cried. "It's as if we're being punished for something by the heavens."

Hearing that made me even more afraid, for I thought if anyone was being punished, it was I. I had disobeyed the father who loved me and petted me and gave me clean water in my bowl and scratched my back. I had left home without a word to anyone. I had broken the promise I had made aboard the first ship to stick to dry land and leave the sea to more experienced sailors.

Terrified, I clung even tighter to the mast when a great shower of hail loosened the grip of my paws. I fell, slamming onto the deck on all fours. I slid hard against the railings as the angry sea splashed over me. The storm was like a living creature, like a raging wild animal. It growled and shouted around us. It pushed and punched at the ship, ramming it against the waves. My coat was wet to the hide, and my paws were bruised and tender. The ocean water splashed on deck with such fury that it knocked me off my four paws.

Suddenly, I heard the shot of a gun. In terror, I put my head down and my tail between my legs.

"The shot is a signal. It means to bail water like crazy," another sailor told me, pulling me up. "Come and help."

I helped the rest of the crew work furiously to keep the ship afloat. We filled buckets with water and dumped them back into the ocean to scoop up more, but still the water flooded the decks.

"I see land!" the first mate called. "But how can that be? I fear we are so far off course that I have no idea where we are at all!"

"Land!" I cried. "Oh, to feel land under my paws!"

Many men lost their courage and screamed, "Help me!" I saw two sailors weeping, clutching frantically at the railing for dear life. The sailor steering the ship grabbed at the wheel again. The wind whipped around him, flinging him away. The wheel cracked in two, with a sound so loud and terrifying that I held my paws over my face.

"We've lost control of the ship!" someone yelled. We watched in horror as the ship sped out of control, heading closer and closer to a great sandbar sticking up out of the water.

"The ship will sink!" someone shouted in horror. "Look! A sandbar! If we strike it, we'll go down for sure!"

In terror, I looked at the sandbar. "Where did that come from?" I shouted. We were swept closer and closer to it. The ship hurtled toward the sandbar and then I shut my eyes. The ship rammed into the sandbar. The jolt knocked me clear across the slippery deck. "We're done for!" I shouted.

Sailors tumbled from the ship, disappearing in the wild, windswept ocean water. Twenty-foot-high waves smashed against the ship.

"Get to the lifeboats!" the captain shouted.

I ran to the side of the ship where the lifeboats were. "We're saved!" I said.

Then I saw that all the lifeboats except one had been smashed by the storm. I crouched, trying to cut with my teeth the ropes that held the last lifeboat. I bit free one side of the lifeboat. I had almost gotten the other side untied when a wave crashed against us.

"Wait!" I cried, water filling my mouth.

I bent down at my task again. This time, however, the next wave grabbed hold of the lifeboat, hitting it with such force that the craft snapped into two pieces.

"We are doomed!" I yelped.

"Abandon ship!" someone cried.

Another sailor leaped over the ship's side and flailed in the storm-tossed water.

"Land, ho!" cried someone else.

"Land what? I don't see any land!" I cried, peering through the squall. "All I see is water as high as mountains!"

Just then I watched, horrified, as the hull of the ship split apart with a resounding *crack*. One by one, the crew members were thrown overboard into the crashing waves.

"Help!" I cried, grabbing a firmer hold on the ship with my paws. A thunderous roar of water splashed over me, tearing my paws from the railing. It pulled me head over tail deep into the sea. I tried to get my bearings, splashing and gulping for air.

Good thing I had those swimming lessons, I thought. I was a strong swimmer, and I dog-paddled as furiously as my four legs would take me. All the while I choked on great gulps of water and spat out as much as I could.

My eyes stung from the salty water. I couldn't see the shore. I couldn't see the captain or the first mate or any of the other sailors.

"Are they all drowned?" I cried. "How can that be?" With every wave that came upon me, I expected to be swallowed up.

I could no longer see my ship. I grew so terrified that I began crying out to the heavens.

"Oh, please, please spare my life, and I promise, if ever I set paws on dry land again, I will go directly home to my father and mother and never climb aboard a ship again. I will never track mud into the house again, but will wipe off my paws! I will never chew shoes—except in an emergency!"

No one could possibly hear me above the roar of the ocean storm, and I was soon sucked deep under the choppy waters.

"Help!" I cried.

Just then I was tossed against a rock. I felt as if I had been struck by a hundred-pound weight. My face and paws were bleeding. The rock was sharp and slippery, but I held on for dear life and dear tail.

"Oh, save me!" I cried. "This time I mean it! Save me, and I won't ever, ever go to sea again! Really! My paws aren't even crossed! I won't even go to the beach! I won't chase after adventure—or even cats!"

But the storm kept up. When I squinted out to sea, I saw the ship was nothing more than a wreck, and all the crewmen were gone! Vanished under the sea!

I held onto the great rock so I would not be tugged back under the raging water. Great waves washed over me. I tried to hold my breath for each of them, but they came so hard and so fast that I continued to swallow great gulps of water. I coughed, desperate and frightened. I was sure I would be washed off the rock and into the ocean at any second. If I wasn't soon eaten by sharks, I would drown. It felt as if I were clinging to the rock for hours and that the storm would never end.

Finally, just as I was almost certain I could not hold on any longer and that all my fur would wash away from my body, the rain stopped and the wind died down.

I rested, recovering some of my strength, and a bit of my courage, too. Shivering and terrified, I shook what water I could from my coat and whiskers. Then I peered out again toward the distance, and lo and behold, I saw land.

"Land!" I cried. "It looks green and habitable! Surely there will be people there, and maybe even a welcoming committee to hail me for surviving such a storm! There will be warm blankets . . . and nourishing food . . . and comfortable clothing . . . and rich soil to dig in . . . and good company!"

The more I thought about the island and its creature comforts, the stronger I felt. I let go of the rock and swam as hard as I could toward the shore. My paws all felt like rubber, as if they couldn't kick an inch more, but I wouldn't stop swimming.

Finally, panting and exhausted, I stumbled onto the sand and collapsed in a heap of wet fur and exhaustion. I fell immediately into a deep sleep.

It was September 30, 1659. Almost a full month after setting sail, I had been shipwrecked.

Chapter Four

Wishbone and Joe stood in the dark living room. "Never fear, Wishbone's here," Wishbone said to Joe. "They don't call me a Seeing Nose Dog for nothing, you know. I can get us out of this."

"What am I going to do about the game? It starts at seven, and it's a quarter to five now," Joe said as he shone the flashlight on his watch again. "I just have to get there. We don't have a lot of time."

Joe eased his way toward the kitchen, the flashlight held firmly in his hand. Wishbone followed closely.

"We'd better take provisions," Joe said. He opened the refrigerator, shining the flashlight into it.

"I'd be glad to help," Wishbone offered.

"Gee, Mom was right. There isn't much food here at all." Joe checked out the shelves. "A jar of pickles, a few slices of cheese . . ."

Joe opened one of the kitchen cabinets and took down a can. He shone his flashlight on it.

"Oh, here's a can of tuna," he said. "But the only can opener we have is the electric one that I bought

Mom for Mother's Day last year. I made her throw the old one out. Come on, Wishbone, let's go get Mom at the dentist's office. It's on the way to the game." Joe squared his shoulders, trying to perk himself up. "It'll be an adventure."

"That's my middle name," said Wishbone.

Wishbone followed Joe outside.

Joe looked around in astonishment. "I'm used to seeing all these houses with lights on," he said. "Without them, it makes it seem as though all these houses are deserted." Joe shook his head. "I thought I'd feel better outside than in the house, but it's even darker out here than it is inside." He glanced up at the sky. "There aren't any stars out tonight. Even the moon is covered by rain clouds." Joe cleared his throat. "I feel as if I have to talk out loud to make sure I'm here. Everything looks so different."

"And it smells different, too, without people around," Wishbone said, lifting his nose up to sniff.

"I don't see any other people around," Joe said. "I don't hear anybody else at all." He shone the flashlight in front of him. "Hello!" Joe called. "Anyone around? It's Joe Talbot!"

The silence felt deafening.

"Hello!" Joe called again. "Anyone out there? This is making me nervous!"

"Any dogs around?" Wishbone barked.

"We'd better get my bike and get going," Joe said. "I don't want to wear out the flashlight batteries before we get to the dentist's office."

Joe went cautiously to the far side of the house and unlocked his bicycle. "At least it's not raining anymore,"

Joe said. He crouched down by Wishbone. "I can tie the flashlight to the handlebar with your leash."

"Take it, take it. My pleasure," Wishbone said. "Consider it a gift."

Joe tied the flashlight to the handlebar and then motioned for Wishbone to follow him. "Okay, we don't have to rush. We have time."

"And we have each other, Joe," Wishbone said.

Joe rode very slowly. "I can hardly see the street," Joe said. He leaned forward and the bike suddenly tilted to the right, bumping over something in the road. "I don't like this at all," Joe said. "I wish we could see some people."

Suddenly, Wishbone began to bark. "I smell something, Joe. Limes—lime aftershave. It's Mr. Pruitt! And I smell hibiscus. That's Wanda Gilmore! Look, over there, Joe! Civilization! We're saved!"

Next door there was a flickering of candles. "Light!" Joe said. "What a relief."

Joe followed the lights. Wanda and Mr. Barnes

37

and a few of the other neighbors were gathered in front of Wanda's house. She had a small table set with candles, a platter of sandwiches, and a pitcher surrounded by waxed-paper cups.

"Halt! Who goes there?" called Wanda, shining a flashlight toward Joe. "Identify yourself."

"It's Joe," Joe said, laughing. "And Wishbone." Wishbone stood on his hind legs.

"Hi, Joe," said Mr. Barnes. "What a night, right?"

"Joe and Wishbone. Hello. Well, it's Wanda, here." Wanda flashed the light toward her own face, and she smiled at Joe. "Just think of the events that are happening even as we stand here. The true adventures of people stranded in darkness, all making the best of a bad situation. True stories of courage and bravery in the face of disaster. It makes you proud to be an Oakdale resident, doesn't it?"

"It makes me proud to be a dog," Wishbone said. Of course, he was always proud of that.

Wanda pointed her camera at Joe. "Come on, Joe, I'll snap your picture. It will be perfect for the blackout article I'll write for the *Chronicle*." She lifted up her camera and tapped it. "Isn't science wonderful? This camera can be used in very low light. You just point it, and it automatically focuses with sonar—the way bats do. Say . . . 'blackout'!" said Wanda, snapping his picture. The flash made Joe blink. Wanda turned to Wishbone. "Say 'milk bone'!" she said. "People love to read about dogs in stories."

"Wait. My left side is my good side," said Wishbone, turning his head.

Wanda put down her camera. She picked up a

plate and offered it to Joe. "Joe, would you care for a blackout sandwich or two?" Wanda said.

"A blackout sandwich?" Joe asked doubtfully.

"Whatever it is, take it!" Wishbone said, moving closer to the table. "I may not know much about the culinary arts, but I know what I like—which is all food."

"Well, in a blackout, you make do with what you have. The problem is," said Wanda, handing him the plate, "I had to make the sandwiches from whatever I had left in the house, so some of them are kind of . . . well . . . creative."

"Creative?" Joe echoed. Then he took a bite. He stopped cold and stared at the sandwich. "What *is* this?" he asked.

"It's very nutritious," Wanda said. "Sardines and peanut butter."

"Uh . . . I guess I'm not that hungry, after all," Joe said. "Anyway, we really have to get going."

"Well, there's also egg salad with mint jelly," Wanda said, fussing with the sandwiches. "It's a very pretty combination." She stared thoughtfully at the plate. "I bet I could put some of these recipes in the *Chronicle,* too." She spread out her hands. "Can't you just see it—Wanda's Blackout Buffet!" She tapped her brow. "I wonder if I have enough ideas for a whole cookbook."

"I'll take some, Wanda!" Wishbone barked. "I can be your official taste tester! I've had lots of experience! Egg salad with mint jelly sounds good to me."

Wanda squinted at Joe. "Let me take your picture again. Look weary and worn out!"

Joe shook his head. "I'm not weary and worn out.

39

I'm excited. Tonight our school league is scheduled to be playing basketball against Oakdale Central Grammar School. And the eighth-grade coach is going to be there. I could be discovered."

Wanda frowned. "In the blackout?"

"Well, maybe Central isn't affected," Joe said. "I bet it isn't."

"Oh, Joe, it looks as if the whole town is in a blackout," Wanda said.

Joe looked alarmed. "The whole town?" he said. "That can't be. There's the game."

"Can't you call someone to find out if it's on?" Wanda said. "I've got my cellular phone here." She picked it up and handed it to Joe.

"Great. I'll call the school." Joe called Information, got the number, then phoned.

"Don't be surprised if no one answers," Wanda said to Joe.

"Personally, I always like to be surprised," Wishbone said.

Joe's face burst into a grin. "Hello?" he said excitedly. "This is Joe Talbot. I'm supposed to be playing at the game tonight. But there's a blackout where I am, and I didn't know whether the game would still be on. . . ." He paused. His smile grew bigger. "It is if enough people show up? Well, count this person in."

"And this dog," Wishbone added.

Joe ended the phone call and gave the phone back to Wanda. "I'm so glad I called." Joe hesitated. "You couldn't give me a lift, could you?"

Wanda patted Joe on the shoulder. "Oh, no one's driving in this darkness."

"That's right, Joe," Mr. Barnes said. "Traffic is snarled for miles."

"But . . . the game!" Joe said with urgency.

Wanda gave Joe an encouraging look. "I'm sure lots of people won't know to show up. I'm sure the schools will reschedule the game."

"No, you don't understand. The game *has* to happen. This is my big chance." Joe looked thoughtful. "I'll just have to bike it," Joe said. "We'll go get Mom at the dentist's."

"I don't think that's such a good idea," Wanda said. She frowned. "Wait a minute, here. I think I just might have an idea that's better."

Joe leaned on his bicycle. "Well, we've got to be going."

"Wait a minute," Wanda said. "I just had a *great* idea. You want fame and adventure? How would you and Wishbone like to be my roving reporters?" said Wanda.

"'Roving' is my middle name," said Wishbone, leaping in midair. "I was born to rove. Just look at this!" He raced across the lawn and then came back.

"I don't know—I have to get to the game," said Joe. "I want to be there early, for pre-game practice."

Wanda put her flash camera into Joe's hands. "Rove the neighborhood and take pictures of the stories as they unfold. Snap the shots that say 'courage and ingenuity.'"

"I guess I could do that on the way." Joe put the camera around his neck. "We're going crosstown to get my mom before we hit the game. There ought to be lots of stories along the way. And I can get my mom to

41

take the winning shot for me." Joe peered down the street. "If only everything wasn't so black!"

"Come on, Joe, let's make some headlines of our own," Wishbone said.

"No, no, stay in the neighborhood," Wanda said. "Your mom will be back soon. Plus, I don't like the idea of you being out there during a blackout. Right here in the neighborhood is much safer. Anyway, the best stories are always the ones right in your own backyard."

"No, no, the *unknown* is always exciting," Wishbone said. "Anything could be right around the next corner."

Joe got on his bike. "Well . . . I don't know about that, Wanda."

"Trust me," Wanda said. "They are. Stick around here." She bit into a sandwich, making a face. "Nutritious," she said firmly, then took another bite. "Anyone want another sandwich?" she asked cheerfully.

Mr. Barnes looked politely away.

"Anyone want a first?" Wanda asked brightly, chewing even more slowly.

Joe rode as slowly as he could, with Wishbone trotting beside him. "I'm not staying right in the neighborhood," Joe said, checking his watch. "Not when my mom is crosstown and it's after five o'clock. Anyway, this is an adventure, right, Wishbone?"

"Adventure calls—Wishbone answers," Wishbone said.

The street was so dark that it was hard to tell where the road turned into sidewalk and where the sidewalk turned into grass. It was quite eerie to see the houses so dark, Wishbone thought.

"We'll see some people soon, I'm sure," Joe said doubtfully.

"Or some dogs," Wishbone said.

But the farther away from the neighborhood Joe and Wishbone got, the darker and more unfamiliar everything seemed. "I know I've ridden my bike down here a zillion times," Joe said, "so why does it look so strange? I wish I could see a landmark or something." He moved the flashlight in a wide arc. "Which direction is the dentist's?" he said. Joe shook his head. He looked up at the sky. "There's not even a moon to light our way."

"I knew we should have joined the Boy Scouts," Wishbone said.

"I should have brought a compass. Then we could figure out which way was north."

Wishbone tilted his head up into the air. "Okay, let's not panic, Joe," Wishbone said. "You forgot—this nose *knows*." Wishbone concentrated. "I'm right here with you. You're lucky to have someone like me." Wishbone lifted his head. "If it has a scent, I can tell you what it is." Wishbone took a practice sniff. "You don't believe me? Well, I'm open to giving free—that's right, free—demonstrations. Watch this."

He smelled the cool night air, the hint of more rain to come. Then suddenly, wafting through, he smelled something familiar, something that he could remember.

"Joe! Joe!" Wishbone said. "I recognize the little

enclosure where all the dogs like to run. I can still smell them. This way. Follow me."

"Wishbone, where are you going?" Joe asked. "Wait. Where are you?"

"I'll just have to sound the alarm," Wishbone said, barking as loudly as he could. "This way, Joe. Shine the flashlight a little to your left and you'll be able to see me."

Joe followed Wishbone to the hydrant, his hand brushing against something. "Wait, I recognize this post. It's got notches in it that one of the kids from school made. If we go left, we should hit the main road."

Just then there was a clap of thunder.

"Oh, great," Joe said. He looked up at the sky just as it began to rain.

Oh, no, it's raining on our parade. We're going to have to be resourceful, just like Crusoe.

Chapter Five

On October 1, 1659, I, Robinson Crusoe, woke up under a sky as brilliantly blue as my favorite food bowl. The sun was beating down and warming me as my blanket at home had done. I bolted upright, terrified to find myself on the island. *I wonder if I am the only one on this island,* I thought.

"Oh, no. This wasn't just a bad dream," I said. I looked toward the ocean. In the distance, to my astonishment, I could still see the wreck of the ship. The ship lay tilted on its side, and there was a great hole torn out of it. The sails, once so proud and billowing, were shredded and plastered against the wood of the ship. "I thought the ship had sunk," I said. "I guess it won't be able to sail anymore."

Glumly, I sank back onto the sand, tucking my tattered tail between my legs. All I could see in the distance were two small islands. They were too far off to swim to, and I couldn't tell whether they were inhabited or not.

"Oh, what am I going to do?" I moaned. "I have no food, no clothing but what is on my back, and no shelter of any kind. Plus, I'm hungry." I looked out at the ocean.

First I thought I must walk about this island and see if anyone else lived on it. Maybe they were farther inland. I imagined a warm house, a clean bed, and a friendly hand to stroke my fur.

I walked deeper into the island's interior. The sandy beach area soon gave way to jungle-like woods, with great, high oak trees and maples and soft, grassy ground. I walked even farther, hoping to find a settlement. Beyond the woods was a valley, lush and green and strewn with wildflowers. "It's pretty," I said. "Pretty lonely. There's no sign of any other person ever being here."

I walked into the valley. There was a fresh-water stream flowing through it. I bent over and lapped at the water, which was cool and clean and delicious. By then, my stomach was growling.

"I'll explore more tomorrow," I said. "For now, I had better head back to the beach, just in case some other survivors have arrived."

When I got back to the shore, however, there was no one to greet me. Sitting on the beach, I stared out at the sea and waited. I was so hungry by then that I could have eaten the very sand itself. I could see the broken ship, which was still floating. I wondered how long it would be there before it sank. How was I going to survive here on this island without food, clothing, or shelter? I stared miserably out at the ship again. And then it hit me!

Suddenly, I remembered all the supplies the crew had put on board before sailing: warm clothing, tools, weapons and ammunition, and food—lots of food. *Not all of it could have washed away in the storm. I'll bet there are lots of supplies still on board,* I thought. *The ship doesn't look that far away now. I could surely dog-paddle right up to it and bring things back that I might need. At least it's a start.* I got up and stretched the last bit of sleepiness from my bones. *I can't believe I'm going back into the ocean, but I can't be a landlubber just yet.*

I took off my clothing. The weather was hot, and now I would have something comfortable and dry to put on when I got back. Finally, I ventured into the same sea where I had almost drowned.

"Be calm, be calm," I told myself. "I'm not afraid . . . not in the least." The water was warm and smooth. It didn't take me long to dog-paddle out to the ship.

Once I got there, however, the problem was how to board the ship.

"It's so high," I said. "Talk about thinking big."

I swam around the ship twice, refusing to give up, getting mouthfuls of salty water that I kept spitting out. The second time I swam around the boat, I spied a small piece of rope hanging from the deck.

"Here goes nothing," I said, grabbing hold of the rope with my teeth.

Fortunately, my grip was strong, thanks to countless games of tug-of-war with socks around my house. In no time at all, I climbed aboard.

"Hello. Anybody here?" I called. The only sound I heard was the splashing of the sea around me. *Then I must be the sole survivor,* I thought.

It was strange to be the only soul aboard the ship.

Every step I took made the wooden deck creak. I was terrified the ship might begin to sink deeper into the ocean. It was dark and eerie where I was. It would probably be even darker under the main deck, but that was where the supplies were.

Carefully, I opened the door that led to the lower decks. I couldn't see a thing. I could hear water sloshing along the bottom of the ship. Every time I took a step, the ship seemed to move. *I had better make this quick,* I thought. *I don't want the ship to sink with me on it.* I stepped down onto the lower deck, soaking my paws.

The open door threw some light down into the lower deck, casting strange shadows. The experience made my fur stand on end. *They're just shadows,* I told myself. For a second, I thought I heard the voice of another sailor, calling me. I was so grateful that I barked my greeting, but it wasn't returned.

"Where are you?" I called. Then the ship was so silent that I realized I must have imagined I had heard anything. The quiet grew so big that I felt swallowed up in it.

I tried to shake off my uneasiness. I quickly went to work, first finding a saw. I held the saw in my mouth and cut pieces of board from the walls and floors of the ship and lashed them together with twine to make a raft. *I never guessed I would ever be a carpenter,* I thought. *But there must be a first time for everything.* I wasn't sure of what I was doing, or if the raft would hold me, but I kept telling myself that I was doing the best I could. When the raft was finished, I was exhausted.

Next, I had to figure out what to load onto it.

There was much to choose from: essentials like food; and items I wanted, like a pretty brass lamp and a set of tin plates.

"I'll keep coming back," I said, "right up until the moment the ship sinks and there is nothing more to take." I shook off my unease like water from my fur. "By the time the food from the ship is gone, hopefully another ship will come and rescue me," I said.

I kept searching the ship. I found three of the seamen's chests and filled them with provisions: bread, rice, dried meat, three Dutch cheeses, and a little bit of corn. I gathered up some clothing, and two pistols I thought might come in handy to hunt wild animals, if there were any, and ammunition. I stopped when I came to a chest that was filled with more gold pieces than I could ever spend.

"Gold!" I cried. "More than I could ever want. I have to take this. I could bring some home to my parents and make amends with it. I could buy a new ship. And a new chew bone!" I dragged everything toward the raft.

I was about to go inspect more of the lower deck when I glanced out to shore and saw that the tide was coming in. "I'd better get going while the going is good," I said, nearly tripping over a broken oar. "What luck. I'd better take this, too."

I gingerly laid two muskets, ammunition, an axe, a sack of corn, a sail, food and clothing, and nails onto the raft.

"It's holding," I said. "Now, let's see if it can support me." Carefully, I made my way onto the raft, one paw at a time. "It's holding!" I cried at each step.

When I finally had all of me—including my tail—on board, I relaxed.

Luckily, the sea was as smooth as a sheet of glass. The wind was blowing gently toward shore. The oar, though broken, worked well enough so I could paddle back to the island.

When I got back to shore, there was a surprise. A fat blond ship's cat sat on the sand, calmly surveying me, licking his paws.

"Where did you come from?" I asked.

The cat did not seem dangerous. I imagined it must have been on one of the ships that had passed the island. Maybe the cat had been used to catch rats on board. The cat had probably swum to shore. *Company,* I thought. *Not my favorite pet, but beggars can't be choosers, I suppose.* I motioned to the cat with one of my front paws.

"My goodness. Cats always smell so fishy. Here, kitty, kitty," I called, but the cat ran away. "What's the matter? Cat got your tongue?" I called.

For the rest of that morning, I unpacked my things. When I saw the gold that I had brought from the ship, I laughed.

"What was I thinking, taking money? What good are you to me now? Can you buy me a home or a snack? It would have been better for me to take more clothing or wood." I pushed at the trunk of coins. "I can't even play a good game of fetch with you. Well, I'll keep you in a safe place. Every time I see you, I'll reflect on the true value of things."

I thought I might get everything else I needed from the ship in a few more trips. Each time I returned

to the vessel, I became so tired that I needed to rest. Whenever I went back to the wreck, I found more and more things that might be useful to me. I found more corn seed, rope, nails, muskets, and more ammunition. Once, I found a pretty glass mirror that I didn't really need, but I wanted it.

Weeks passed, and then, to my surprise, months. Finally, when I last checked my makeshift calendar, six whole months had passed—six months, and no one had come to rescue me! How could that be?

After all that time, the ship seemed to have sunk down a little more. There seemed to be more water in the cabins belowdecks. There were more strange sounds on the boat that I couldn't recognize. At times, I was sure the vessel was haunted.

In between the trips I took to the wrecked ship, I began to survey the island. It was lush and green and seemed to have plenty of good places to dig. I worried about what wild animals I might run into. As I walked deep into the jungle land, however, the only other animals I saw were wild goats and some parrots.

"Great. Goats. Maybe I can milk them," I told myself. "All I have to do is figure out how to catch them." Maybe I could trap them with some of the rope I had brought ashore. Maybe I could spare a bit of food to use as bait—like some of those corn kernels I had brought back. I cut a length of rope, forming a collar. "I'll try to catch some goats tomorrow."

I wandered around until I found a spot that seemed green and shady.

"Okay, now to find temporary shelter," I said. "But how? And where?"

I surveyed my piles of supplies. There was the hammock I had taken from the ship. It would make a fine bed. I also had a good length of strong sail. I pulled out the sail. *It would make a good tent,* I thought. I tied it onto two high tree branches. By the time I had finished, I was so exhausted that all I wanted to do was sleep. Just then I heard a crackling noise.

"I hope it's not wild animals," I said.

Chapter Six

I listened for wild animals all that night, but I seemed to be safe. I lay with my golden wealth secure. That night a storm blew up, but I was dry and warm inside my tent.

In the morning, when I awoke, the rain was gone, and so was some of the stiffness in my four legs. I looked out to sea, but I couldn't see the ship any longer. *The storm must have either sunk it or blown it out to sea,* I thought. I had seen the wrecked ship every day for six months. Not seeing the ship made me feel lonelier than ever. The ocean had a strange, eerie peacefulness to it. It was bright blue and smooth and calm.

That day, I thought I'd explore another side of the island. Half the time I was yearning to find someone else on the island. But half the time I was afraid of what I might find. The people could be savages! To keep up my courage, I barked every now and again as I walked, heading toward a rockier coastline, which broke off into two broad hills. I spent half the day climbing the hills. When I got to the top, I could see the whole island. "Nothing but land," I said. "I don't see signs of any other person."

Now I am really alone, I thought, beginning to get scared. *Who will I talk to? What will I do? Who will scratch me behind my ears? The food from the ship won't last forever. Have I just been saved to die a terrible death here alone and helpless?* I became so afraid that I thought I'd have to do something to keep my spirits up.

I remembered how it was for me when I was at home and it had stormed, and I threw back my head and howled the way I used to, which always made me feel more cheerful. I chased my tail for good measure. Then I recited poems that I had memorized, many of them pure doggerel. Finally, I decided to keep a written record of my adventures, hoping that I might someday be rescued. I got out the pen and ink and paper that I had taken from the ship. After putting the pen in my mouth, I soon made a list of what I felt was bad and what was good about my situation:

BAD

I am shipwrecked on a lonely island.

I have no more clothes.

There is a cat here.

I have no food I really like.

The living accommodations are not first-class.

I may never be rescued.

I have only an old chew bone.

GOOD
I am alive and not drowned, as all my shipmates were.
I am healthy and am cast away on an island where
    I see no wild beasts to hurt me.
I don't have to have a flea bath.
I can find food.
I have built shelter.
I have a chew bone.
There is a cat to chase.

I kept reading my list over and over until it made me feel just a bit better.

That night, I was freezing cold in my tent. I was also very uncomfortable sleeping on the grass. *Any wild animal could tear this tent apart,* I thought, beginning to get frightened. I had grown up with all the comforts. I had not trained to live in the wilderness, but I would have to learn how now.

"I've got only my wits and what I took from the wrecked ship to help me survive. I can't give up. If I do, I will die," I told myself.

The next day, I began to look for someplace to build a more permanent home. *A fortress would be more like it,* I thought.

I knew I needed fresh water. I also knew I needed to be someplace far enough away from the ocean so that the tide could not wash me away. I did want to be close enough to the sea, so that if rescue came, the sailors would see my wagging tail.

I began to walk across the island. I soon found a green patch of land on a little rising hill. "This looks perfect," I said. "What great digging space. Talk about your prime real estate." I was so happy I rolled around and around in the grass before I pitched my tent.

I began to build a small house, trying to make it like a kind of fort. I used the wood and nails I had taken from the ship. I worked slowly, doing a little bit each day, until I was so exhausted that I curled up right where I was and fell asleep.

Building my house took me much longer than I thought it would. I had passed one year on the island, and it was only half finished. "At least this is keeping me busy while I wait for rescue," I told myself.

I didn't have much time to worry about my situation. At night, I was so tired that I fell instantly asleep the moment I lay down. As soon as I woke up, I had to start work again.

During the second year of house construction, I thatched the roof with tall grasses I pulled out of the ground with my teeth. "That will keep it waterproof," I told myself.

I made one window so I could see outside.

"Ah, a window shade!" I said, plucking a broad leaf from a tree. I fastened it onto the top of the window with a nail. I could lift it and lower it when I pleased.

Inside my home was a dirt floor that I ached to dig in, but I resisted. *I will have to cover it up. And I have to build a table and a chair and a bed,* I thought.

I went outside again and began digging a deep cave behind my home for storage of my supplies. I scratched deep into the ground, using all four paws.

"My stomach is growling," I said. "What I need is a kitchen—someplace convenient, but not so close to the house that I could burn down my sleeping quarters or draw too many animals near." I imagined the meals I might cook. But I had seen enough of the island now to know that nothing my mouth watered for—meat stew or kibble—seemed available to me here.

It wasn't until my home was completed that I realized how much more time had gone by.

"I've been on this wretched island for two and a half years," I said. The very thought of it made me feel so hopeless that I lay down, wrapping my tail around my body for comfort.

A safe home was one thing; loneliness was another. Although occasionally I saw a wild cat or some goats, I longed for the sound of another voice. The silence was so complete that it was deafening. "Well, I have lungs. I could use them," I said. I continued talking aloud to myself the whole day long. I told myself what I was doing. "Now I'm biting a tick on my fur. Now I'm licking my paw," I said.

I described parts of the island out loud, paying particular attention to the best digging areas. Although I couldn't really carry a tune very well, I sang all the songs I knew, over and over again, from rousing sea shanties to melodies so beautiful they brought a tear to my eye and a wag to my tail.

I've got to be careful or I will go crazy from being alone, I thought. I continued to keep a list of what was bad and what was good about the island. Then I decided that I should keep a journal of my time there to hold my spirits up. I took out the notebook and a pen I had found on the ship. I made myself comfortable under a leafy tree. Then I began to write:

On September 30th, 1659, I, poor, miserable Robinson Crusoe, became shipwrecked during a dreadful storm and came ashore on this dismal, unfortunate island. Everyone else was drowned.

I read over what I had written. It made me feel a little better, a little less alone. I was used to leaving my mark in places—muddy prints on a clean floor, creative landscaping in the neighbor's garden, but this situation was going to call for something more. *I can make my presence known in other ways, as well,* I thought.

I stood up and walked to a large tree. I had a knife with me, and I grasped it in my mouth. "I'll keep track of my time here this way, by marking each day I am forced to be here right on this tree," I said. "I can't rely on my memory. This way, if and when I run out of ink, I can still know how long I have been here on this island." I cut a deep notch as carefully as I could. Then I carved the words:

I CAME ONSHORE HERE THE 30TH OF SEPTEMBER, 1659. TWO AND A HALF YEARS HAVE SINCE PASSED.

I stood back, surveying my work. "There," I said with great satisfaction. "Now, every week I shall remember to carve another notch."

Boy, that Robinson Crusoe sure has the write stuff, doesn't he? I myself always leave my signature and sign my work—like my paw prints on Ellen's kitchen floor! Unfortunately, my genius—unlike Crusoe's—isn't appreciated!

Chapter Seven

Another year passed. I had carved so many notches into the tree that I had to create a new calendar on a new tree. One more year! I couldn't believe it. I had now been on the island three and a half years. I never gave up hope that someone would come and rescue me, but I could not spend all my time staring out to sea waiting for a ship. I had to take care of myself. Every passing day reminded me of what I didn't have. While I watched my clothing decay from wear, I thought that if I did not have warm clothes, I could get sick. As the food supplies from the ship dwindled, I knew that if I did not have food, I would surely die.

I had been a reckless youth who ran off to sea, but now I had to be anything but reckless if I wanted to survive. I had to plan. I rationed the food I had taken from the ship. I let myself have only one meal a day, usually a bit of the dried meat I had brought to shore. I began to panic at the thought of my food running out. "What will I do when the rest of my food is gone?"

It didn't take long for that to happen. In six more months, all food was gone.

I was terrified. I began walking for longer and longer amounts of time in the jungle, trying to find something to eat. The goats were now so used to me that they suddenly came out when I was around.

"Now is the time to catch one of the goats. Goats give milk," I told myself. I took some of the rope I had brought from the ship. The goat was easy enough to catch. I pulled it along by the rope, held in my mouth.

I was not paying much attention. Suddenly I noticed it didn't feel as if I was pulling anything. I turned around and looked down at a strip of rope that was chewed off at the end. The goat must have eaten it and then vanished.

The next day, I returned to the goats. "If the goats won't come to me, I will go to them," I said. I approached a goat. The goat let me milk him, and finally my belly was full. Still, I felt this was only temporary. What if I couldn't find a goat to milk or keep it still enough to milk it later on?

I watched the goat to see what plants it liked to eat. I followed it to some grapevines on the other side of the island. I had noticed them before, but this was the first time they actually had grapes growing on them.

"This is great!" I cried. "Now I can put the grapes around my home to keep the goat there so I can milk it. Better than that, I can even have lots of grapes for myself, too."

I took pawfuls of grapes home. The goat followed me, and the grapes it didn't eat quickly began to rot. *This is no good,* I thought. *I need things that might last.* It suddenly dawned on me. I could dry the grapes in the sun and have raisins.

I went back to the vines and began picking the grapes, but another problem arose. Without a basket to place them in, the process of carrying the grapes to a field and then spreading the grapes out to dry and then bringing them back to my home took days.

I needed baskets. I knew baskets were woven, but what could I use to weave one? I searched around the island and suddenly came upon a tree with long, thin, supple twigs. I picked off as many twigs as I could carry and sat down, trying to figure out how to weave. I made four attempts before I learned how to weave a basket. It took me three days to finish it. When the basket was completed, it certainly wasn't beautiful. It did not look like any basket I'd ever seen in the shops of London. "But who cares?" I said. "It can hold grapes and raisins." I was as happy as if someone had presented me with a brand-new ball to fetch.

I went back to the grapevines and picked enough grapes to dry in the sun. When they were dried into raisins, I barked happily.

"Now I will always have a supply of food!" I said with joy.

I had something to carry solid things in, but a basket wouldn't hold water. What was I to do when I woke up in the middle of the night thirsty? It was too far and too dark to walk all the way to the spring for water. Many a night I lay awake thirsty. I didn't know what I would do until one day, on one of my walks, I found some clay in the ground. I dug at it with my paws and then tried to shape it into a kind of pot.

"This isn't too bad," I told myself.

But once the pot had been made, the clay had to be heated to become a hard pot. Unfortunately, I did not have an oven. But I did have fire. I rubbed two sticks together until they set off a spark. I blew on the spark until it turned into a fire. Then I put the clay pot into it. To my great surprise, the fire hardened the clay.

I carried the pot to the stream and filled it with water. That night, when I woke up thirsty, I took a quick drink and then fell back to sleep. The next morning, I was also able to wash myself without having to walk all the way to the stream first.

Over the next two years that followed, I made other items that would make my life more comfortable. I drove the few nails I had taken from the ship into some rock, using a hard piece of wood as a hammer. *Now I can hang things from these nails,* I thought proudly. I brought a pot of water and a basket of raisins to my home, and they gave me great pleasure.

My clothing was now so threadbare that I knew I would have to do something. Although the island was rather hot, I couldn't go naked. My skin was too fair, and already I was suffering from sunburn. I was also getting eaten alive by the insects. I needed clothing for protection.

I wasn't sure what to do about this problem. One

day, I was looking around the island when I came upon a goat that had died. *Goatskin!* I suddenly thought. *I can skin the goat and use its hide as clothing!*

It was difficult to do tasks without the right tools. I didn't have a hammer. I looked around in despair and then had an idea. "Trees!" I said. "I can cut one down and make tools from the hard wood." I got my axe and struck at one of the trees until I had felled it. Then I cut a long piece from it, striking at it with my axe, until it was thinner and thinner. Finally, I had made myself a kind of wooden knife.

I skinned the goat carefully and then put the skin out on the beach to tan and soften. This process took a week. When the skin was soft, I cut it with my knife and fashioned it into a jacket and pants that I sewed

together with strips of goatskin. I was careful to leave five holes—four were for my paws, and one for my tail.

I was so careful in doing my work that I even had enough hide left over to make an umbrella. "Now the sun won't burn my fur," I said happily. "And I can keep the rain from soaking me." My clothing felt light and comfortable. "Maybe I won't win a beauty contest, but so what?" I said. I felt a great sense of relief to have decent clothes. I knew that there were more goats, so I could manage to have a new suit of clothing whenever I needed one.

I was warm, dry, and splendid in my new outfit. I smoothed my paws down on my new clothes. I wandered down to the water and stared at my reflection.

"You handsome devil!" I exclaimed. I barked out a laugh, I was so happy. My eyes were bright, my whiskers perky.

Another year passed. I still had not given up hope of being rescued. Every night I continued to light a fire so a passing ship might see it. "All good things come to those who wait," I told myself. "Like a scratch behind the ears after a hard day."

But I couldn't just wait. I began building a small canoe, using my saw and the hard woods that were a half mile inland from the shore.

It took me nearly two months to make the boat. When I was finished, even though the boat was small, it was so heavy that I could not move it into the water. I sat in front of the boat, thinking about all the time I had wasted building it. "Wait," I told myself sternly. "Think of this as a valuable lesson. Next time, plan before you build anything. And find a lighter wood."

The matter of food was another thing I worried over. I had enough goat's milk and raisins, but I was tired of dining on them.

"Surely it can't be healthy just to eat two kinds of things," I said. Every day I scoured the island looking for something else that I could eat. The grapevines began to wilt, which set me chasing my tail in panic. I couldn't live on just goat's milk. And the goats were my only company. I couldn't kill them for meat.

What am I going to do? I thought. When I put on my goatskin clothes, they began to hang loosely about my paws.

"I'm losing weight," I said. "This is not good. I need to be as strong as a pit bull if I want to survive."

One day, I was walking across the island, worrying about where my next meal might come from, my belly rumbling with hunger. I was staring down at the ground, thinking about all the bones I had buried in back of my house in London.

"How far away that seems now," I said. "It seems as useless to think about it as it would be to teach a poodle to dance."

I was walking back to my island home when, to my absolute amazement, I saw several tiny green shoots of corn sprouting up.

"Is this a dream?" I cried, stooping to sniff the crop. Then I remembered all the things I had taken from the ship and how I had tossed the corn kernels to bait the goats. "The corn must have just grown without my even knowing it! But why now? What happened? How can I make sure it will still grow?" I shook my head in wonder and licked my chops in anticipation. I was so relieved I nearly wept. "Corn!" I barked. "Now I'm to be a farmer, as well as a builder. Maybe I can even have popcorn!"

I quickly began to think about how I could fill a pail with water and carry it in my mouth to nourish this crop. I wondered how I might learn the best way to keep my corn flourishing. And I thought about how I might even grind it in my teeth and bake it in my fire to make myself biscuits.

"It's something to look forward to, and that means hope," I told myself. Instantly, my spirits rose, and my tail began to wag.

But even the best-laid plans can sometimes go awry. On June 18, I woke up very ill. My normally cold nose was hot with fever. My usually bright eyes were bloodshot, and my fur was clammy on my hide.

"What do I do now, without medicine or warm blankets? What do I do without a comforting hand to pet me?" I moaned. I was frightened almost to death. I lay down in my house and soon fell into a deep, feverish sleep.

I had a terrible dream in which a man standing in a bright flame of fire came to me. I was astonished.

The man pointed accusingly at me. "You disobeyed your father!" he cried to me. "You thought only of your own wealth and fame! That is why you are now sick! You are not grateful enough! You should be sitting up and begging for mercy!"

I was terrified. The man lifted up a spear to me,

and I awoke, shivering, my fur damp with sweat. Immediately I got up and wrote down everything that had happened in the dream. I hoped that writing it down would make the horror I felt go away.

Dream or no dream, it still seemed very real, I scribbled in my notebook.

Uneasily, I began to think about what I should be grateful for again. This time, my list was a lot bigger than the first. I now had a corn crop, goats, a table and chair, a warm place to sleep—and I was alive. I had no fleas and no burrs matted in my fur.

"It was only a dream," I kept repeating. "And I'm grateful. I'm grateful!"

It took a while, but I was able to shake off the nightmarish dream. Every single day after that, I wrote down what I was grateful for.

Gradually, as I got better and better at making things, I began to take satisfaction in the simple things. My home might not be as grand as any in London, but it was warm and comfortable. My food might not be like my mother's delicious cooking, but it was filling and sometimes even tasty.

Time passed, and after eight years on the island, I began to take pride in all that I could do for myself. What was missing was food for my soul.

"I need a friend!" I cried. "I need someone to talk to. Someone. Anyone. No experience necessary."

Crusoe's wish would be granted—but in a surprising way, and not until years later.

Chapter Eight

Time crept up on me as silently and sneakily as a cat. I saw by the notches on the trees that I had been on the island for eleven years and six months. "How can it be that I have been here this long?" I cried. "Why has a ship not passed by? I have been grateful; I have changed. But all these years of loneliness are more than enough, thank you. It is time now to feed the soul, as well as the body."

I thought of my poor father and mother. *They must miss me. They must think I care little for them not to be in contact.* I wept when I thought that, because it surely wasn't true.

One day, I was deep in the woods walking when I heard something whistling. "Am I hearing things, or is this a real whistle?" I said to myself.

My heart jumped with a feeling of excitement, and my whiskers sprang to attention.

"Hello!" I called. "Who's there?" I was so excited

that my tail was wagging so hard I thought it might fall off. I might have a dining companion! I might have someone to take walks with.

My loneliness is at an end at last, I thought. *But who is it, and how did they get onto the island? And, more important, are they friendly?*

"Come out, come out, whoever you are!" I said. I looked around. "Don't be shy." I walked closer to the source of the whistling. "Please come out!" I barked.

Suddenly I spied a brightly plumed parrot perched in a tree. I had seen parrots before. They were always silent and very pretty, much like this one. *That might make a good present for my guest,* I thought.

The parrot suddenly whistled.

I froze in place.

The parrot whistled again.

"You are the one who whistled? You are my company?" I said, bewildered.

My hopes were dashed. I felt myself sinking into unhappiness.

"Wait a minute," I told myself. "So it isn't what I had expected. Haven't I learned to be grateful for the smaller things? What's smaller around here than a parrot? At least it is a living thing. It can be a source of company for me."

Its feathers were red and blue and a beautiful yellow. It had a beak as deep brown as the mud puddles that I loved to roll in.

"Polly want a milk bone?" I asked, trying to get it to talk.

The bird seemed friendly enough, and I was

thrilled to hear its whistle. I put out my front paw, encouraging the parrot to perch.

"Come on, I don't bite," I assured the bird. "And I've had all my shots."

The parrot flew toward me, landing on my paw.

"'Atta bird," I said soothingly. "Come on home with me," I urged.

The bird fluttered its wings, then settled itself on my back, and together we walked home.

I had often chased birds, but never pampered one, as I did this parrot. I built it a wood perch, feeding it some of the seed from the corn I had planted.

"I'll call you Poll, if you have no objections," I said. "If you prefer another name—Sam, Bill, Fido—then you had better tell me right now." When the bird

merely blinked at me, I took that to be an agreement. "Poll, it is, then," I said.

Poll soon became mighty well acquainted with me. I spent months trying to teach Poll to talk.

"Polly want a milk bone?" I repeated over and over, as patiently as if I were teaching it to sit or fetch, or a number of tasks I prided myself on being able to do on command.

Unfortunately, the parrot stayed silent. *Oh, well,* I thought, *at least the parrot can keep me company.* Still, every day, I walked by the bird and tried to get it to say a few simple phrases. Every day I walked away, muttering to myself.

One night I was sleeping when I was startled awake by a voice. "Poor Robinson Crusoe! Where are you? Where have you been? Poor Robinson Crusoe!" the voice sang out.

"Who's there?" I called. "Friend or foe?" My heart hammered within me. I had been on the island for almost twelve years without hearing another voice. I tried to look around and see where that voice was coming from, but all I saw were trees. "Who is there?" I said again. I was so terrified that my tail stood straight up.

Who does that voice belong to? You know, sometimes having company can be as scary as being alone—especially in the wilderness.

Chapter Nine

Joe and Wishbone headed across town toward Ellen. Joe stopped when they got to Forrest Lane. He tied the flashlight more tightly onto his handlebar, studying the thin beam. "It's still holding out," he said. Joe tapped his head. "A flashlight headlight. That's using the old noggin," he said. "Champs need to exercise their minds just as much as they do their bodies."

"And their stomachs!" Wishbone declared. "Are you getting hungry, Joe?"

Joe checked his watch. "We don't have that much time," he said. "It's already five-thirty."

The streets of Oakdale were clogged with traffic. The car horns were beeping so loudly and so often that the noise created a weird kind of music. Some of the cars were blocking the crosswalks. A few had stopped at the side of the road.

"All these cars, and not one of them is moving fast enough to chase," Wishbone marveled. One car honked its horn loudly. "Sorry, I don't speak your language," Wishbone said to the car.

Just then, Joe stopped. "I hear something over all of these horns," he said. "Someone's crying. But where?"

Wishbone heard it, too. He sniffed at the air. "It smells like—it smells like crayons! It's a little kid!" He sniffed at the air again. "It's a . . . a little girl . . . about seven years old."

Joe strained to see over the traffic. The crying continued. "At least we have the light from the headlights to help us," Joe said. He stood up on his bike.

Wishbone took another, longer sniff. "It's over here, Joe," he said, "past the road in the woods." He darted away from Joe and started to cross the busy street, toward the wooded area. Drivers honked their horns angrily.

"Wishbone!" Joe called. "Wishbone, come back. We don't have time for this."

"Follow me, Joe," Wishbone called. "Follow my bark."

He waited, watching Joe maneuver through the lines of cars, weaving his bike through the traffic. When he got to Wishbone, he was panting. "Wishbone, don't do that again," Joe said.

Joe suddenly was silent. The crying was louder.

"Who's there?" Joe called. "Do you need help?"

The crying grew even louder. Joe shined his light into the darkness. He lit up the base of a tree, and then a patch of grass.

"Help!" someone called.

"I don't see anyone," Joe said, shining the flashlight wildly.

Joe and Wishbone continued to move deeper into

the neighborhood, following the cry. They reached a street that was completely deserted.

"Boy, is this dark," Joe said.

He moved forward.

"The crying is coming from over there," he said, when suddenly he stumbled right onto a pair of small white sneakers. "Hey!" Joe said, aiming the light up. He saw a blue dress and blond hair and green eyes. "It's a little girl," Joe said. "She looks as if she's about nine—"

"Seven," said the girl.

"Told you," Wishbone said.

She had blond braids and she was sitting down, rubbing her eyes and crying. "I was on my way home with my older sister when I wandered off. Then I tripped in the dark. I hurt my ankle. I can't walk on it."

"I can't stand to see anyone cry," Wishbone said, then licked her face. "Allow me to introduce myself. Wishbone, at your service."

Joe crouched down by the little girl. "Where do you live?" he asked.

"At two-oh-two Temple Lane," she said. "And my name is Sara."

"Temple Lane," Joe said. "That's really far from here."

Sara looked as if she were going to cry. "Are you going to leave me here?" she asked, sobbing.

"Of course not," Joe said quickly. "Can you walk if you lean on me?"

Sara tried to stand and instantly crumpled back to the ground.

"Okay, what if I put you on the bike and we can wheel you?" Joe suggested.

Sara sniffled.

"Come on, give it a try," Joe said.

Wishbone licked her hand. "In case you didn't know, this is the international symbol of friendship," he said.

Instantly, Sara relaxed a little. She reached for Joe's hand. "What's the dog's name?"

"Wishbone," Joe said.

He helped Sara onto the bike, steadying her with his hands, but she was too upset. The bike was too wobbly, even with Joe trying to balance it.

"Okay, we'll think of something else," Joe said. He looked down at his watch worriedly.

"Do you have to go somewhere?" Sara asked. "Are you going to leave me alone?" She looked as if she were about to cry again.

"I told you I wouldn't," Joe said quickly. "Don't worry. We'll get you home."

Joe looks really worried about the time, Wishbone thought. *I have to come to his rescue!* Wishbone sniffed at the air. "Joe, I have an idea," he barked.

"Nice doggie," said Sara.

"And smart, too," Wishbone said. He rubbed at one of Joe's pants legs, moving him to the right.

"Wishbone, come on. We don't have time to play tug-of-war," Joe said.

"I guess I have to play the dog version of show-and-tell," Wishbone said. "Joe! Yoo-hoo! Over here to the right. Look what I'm showing you." Wishbone barked and ran to the right.

"There's nothing over there, Wishbone—nothing but the supermarket." Joe suddenly stopped in his tracks. "The supermarket!" he said. "I bet there are some shopping carts left outside." He looked down at Sara. "We could borrow one and wheel you in it. Maybe by the time I go get one and get back here, you'll think of a shortcut we can take. Then we can get you home quickly. Then I'll return the cart, and Wishbone and I can be on our way." He peered at his watch. "If we hurry, I could get to the dentist's and the game."

"A shopping cart?" Sara said doubtfully. "What game?" She looked anxious.

"Everything is going to be fine. Will you be okay if Wishbone stays with you for a moment while I get a cart?" Joe asked. "I have to take the flashlight, so it might be really dark when I leave." Sara nodded and put her hand on Wishbone's head. "Wishbone, you bark when I call you, so I know where you are," Joe said.

It didn't take Joe very long to get a cart. Wishbone heard the squeaky wheels before he saw them. "Joe!" he barked. "Over here!"

"Okay, here we go," Joe said. "There were lots of carts." He lifted Sara up and settled her into the shopping cart. "Perfect," he said.

Joe checked his watch again. He began to wheel the cart a little faster, holding onto his bike with his other hand.

"We'll get you home. Don't worry."

"Don't *you* worry, Joe!" Wishbone said. "Things will work out."

Wishbone, Joe, and Sara moved deeper into the town, heading onto Oak Street.

It's so dark," Sara said breathlessly. She held on tightly to the shopping cart, and to Wishbone, who had decided to sit with her to keep her company.

"Wow! You've got some tight grip," Wishbone said to Sara.

As they got near Sara's neighborhood, the streets looked even more deserted.

"The blackout is in this part of town, too?" Joe asked. "It can't be in the *whole* town, can it?"

He looked up at the office buildings, which were dark and empty-looking. There was almost no sound on the street, except for the squeaky wheels of the borrowed shopping cart.

Joe scouted the streets, checking his watch by shining the flashlight on it. "I didn't think wheeling a shopping cart and a bike together would take so much time," he said.

There was a sudden roaring *boom* of thunder. Then a flash of lightning quickly lit up the sky. Sara cringed.

"Don't be afraid," Wishbone said, licking her hand.

"That was close!" Joe said. "Please don't rain," he said, looking at the sky.

The thunder boomed again.

"Too close," Wishbone said.

"There's the street," Joe said. "Now, where is your house?"

Sara pointed.

Joe wheeled the cart all the way to the front door, as fast as he could. He rang the bell. In just moments, a worried-looking woman opened the door. "Sara!" she cried. "Thank goodness. You can't know how worried we've been. Your father and sister are out searching for you." The woman looked at Joe and Wishbone. "Thank you so much for bringing her home."

"It's all right," Joe said.

"My pleasure," said Wishbone.

"Come back and visit anytime," Sara said, patting Wishbone. "Do you want to come in for cake?"

"We have to be someplace right away, but thank you for your offer, anyway," Joe said.

"Can we ask for a doggie bag?" Wishbone said hopefully.

Joe and Wishbone made their way back to the supermarket to return the shopping cart. "Why does it seem as if it's taking longer going back?" Joe said. "The cart is lighter without Sara and you in it, so the trip should be easier." He looked around. "I'm getting really tired," he admitted. "I didn't realize a little girl and a dog could be so heavy to wheel."

By the time they got back to the supermarket, Joe was walking slower than ever. He put the shopping cart back by the market and then got on his bike.

"It's really late now," Joe said. "It's six o'clock already! We really have to hurry to get Mom. I hope she's still at the dentist's."

Joe rode his bike. "What a relief to ride instead of walk," he said. "But I still feel as if I'm moving really slowly."

"I don't mind walking after that cart ride, Joe," Wishbone said.

Joe pedaled faster, deeper and deeper into the town. He looked up at the dark buildings, and at the empty street. "I thought for sure that this part of town would have some lights," he said. "Well, I hope that changes fast. It'll be great not to have to squint in the dark anymore."

When they reached the dentist's block, the town was still dark.

Joe stopped his bike. "What is going on here?" he asked. He squinted into the darkness. "Mom always parks right by the office. That's odd. I don't see any sign of her car."

Wishbone sniffed at the air. "I don't catch her

scent, either," Wishbone said. He held his head up and sniffed again. "I don't catch *anyone's* scent."

Joe pedaled up to the dentist's office. "We didn't get here a moment too soon. I don't think I could have biked a block more." He stopped in front of the dentist's office. He looked horrified.

"Uh-oh." Wishbone barked. "The lights aren't on, and it seems as if nobody's home."

"It's completely dark!" Joe exclaimed. "But wait. What's that taped on the door? It looks like a note!" Joe grabbed it and shone his flashlight on it. "It's from Mom—"

"What does it say?" Wishbone asked.

"It says, 'Joe, sorry we got cut off on the phone. Just in case you come looking for me, I'm taking a taxi home to pick you up and give you a lift if the game is on. Love, Mom.'

"Home?" Joe said. "We don't have time to go back home. It's already six-fifteen. Wishbone, we've got to keep going."

Chapter Ten

"Let's find a phone and call the school," Joe said to Wishbone. "I want to be absolutely sure that the game is still on."

"There's a phone over there," Wishbone said, "right over by that corner."

Joe walked over to the phone and dialed the school. "It's ringing," Joe said. "Come on, someone, pick up. Pick up the line."

"Isn't there anyone over there good at fetching the phone?" Wishbone asked.

"Hello?" Joe said excitedly. "Ronny. You made it to the game. . . . No, no, I'm not at home. There was a blackout in my neighborhood. I went to meet my mom at the dentist's office, but she's already left. . . . What? . . ." Joe frowned.

"Uh-oh, Joe, I don't like the face you have on right now," Wishbone said. "The last time I saw that face, you had to stay inside and do a history report when we were supposed to go for a run in the park. What's wrong, Joe?"

"What about Tony? Didn't he show up? . . . And

Tom didn't make it, either? . . ." Joe ran his hand over his face. "No, we can't forfeit the game. I know you want the coach to notice you, too. It's up to me, then. . . . Of course I'll be there. You can count on it." Joe hung up the phone. "If I don't show up, they'll be one player short and have to forfeit the game." Joe looked at his watch. "It's six-fifteen already. How are we ever going to do it?"

"Joe, take it easy," Wishbone urged. "Let's figure this out together."

"Okay," Joe said. "If I don't go, my team forfeits the game. That's bad. If I go, I play the worst I've ever played in my whole life. The eighth-grade coach will see me do it. That's bad, too. My team might lose on account on me. That's even worse."

Joe paced the sidewalk.

"If I do go, my team gets to play. That's good. Maybe they can even win. That's even better." Joe sighed. "I don't know what to do. I don't know what's going to happen, and whether it's better to go or not to go. Maybe we should just head back home."

"Joe, don't give up," Wishbone said. "Remember that time I was sure I couldn't muster enough strength for a third game of fetch, but I did? Boy, that turned out to be one of my best Saturdays."

Joe squinted at his watch in the dimming beam of light coming from the flashlight. "I can't let my team down. I have to be at the game, tired or not. I have to play. We have to get there."

"Where there's a will, there's a wag," Wishbone said, wagging his tail. "I can cheer you on."

Just then, the flashlight tied to Joe's handlebar

flickered and then went out. The road was now completely dark. "Oh, no!" Joe tapped the flashlight against the handlebar. "Sometimes if you jiggle it, you can start it up again." He picked up the flashlight and shook it, but it stayed dark. "And sometimes, you can't," Joe said glumly. "The batteries must be dead."

"Uh . . . Joe," said Wishbone, "does this mean what I think it does?"

"There's not even anyone around," Joe said. "This is terrible. How are we going to see well enough to get to the game?" He tied the flashlight back on the handlebar of his bike. "Well, we'll have to be careful. We'll have to keep calm, too. That's the important thing."

"Well, dark or not, remember, this nose knows," Wishbone said. "Follow me. Stay close, Joe." He wound himself around Joe's legs. "Using my keen canine sense of smell, I'll have us to the game in no time."

"Wishbone, nothing looks very familiar." Joe followed Wishbone and then brightened a bit. "Wait! Jackson Park is right over there. If we keep to the path, we can take a shortcut and be at the school in time for the game!"

Joe and Wishbone stopped before they entered the park. The trees cast so much of a shadow that it was impossible to see the pebble path that Joe usually took.

"Gee, it's dark," Joe said uncertainly. "Too dark to bike, I think. And it's so quiet, it's a little bit creepy." He reached for Wishbone.

"I'm right beside you, Joe," Wishbone said. "Just watch where you walk. You wouldn't want to step on the dog."

"Maybe our eyes just have to get used to the dark a little bit," Joe said.

He took a tentative step forward. His sneakers crunched on the pebbly path.

"This isn't so scary," Joe insisted, making his voice as loud and strong as he could. "All we have to do is stick to the path."

"Like fur on a dog," Wishbone said.

Something rustled in the distance. Joe stopped. "That's just the wind blowing through a tree," he said hesitantly. He peered forward. "Isn't it?"

"Sure it is, Joe. What else could it be?" Wishbone said.

Joe took a few steps forward. "I'm only going slowly because I don't want to trip and miss the big game," he said. Suddenly, he bumped into a tree. "Ow!" Joe cried, rubbing his shoulder.

"Joe, stay close to me," Wishbone said.

"Maybe this shortcut was a bad idea," Joe admitted. He sighed.

Just then, a sound split the silent night.

"What was that?" Joe stopped so short that he bumped into Wishbone.

"Sounds like—" Wishbone said. Then he felt something prickling up along his fur. "Sounds as if it's coming closer."

"Stay still," Joe said. The two of them became like statues. Then the sound sharpened into a loud, booming bark. "Oh, no, I don't like the sound of that bark. We don't have the time for this," Joe said, "or the strength."

Wishbone froze.

"Oh, no. I recognize that sound. Danger has a new name," Wishbone said. "And it's Bruno the Doberman!"

It seems as if Joe and I are about to be in *big* trouble—big, as in Bruno! Bruno is a dog so nasty that he growls even when he's happy, which is just about never! It's already six-thirty, and this is the last thing we need to hold us up. And talk about danger—who *was* that voice calling out to Crusoe in our story? Let's wag on over and see!

Chapter Eleven

"**P**oor Robinson Crusoe," the voice wailed. Terrified, I began to get up. I moved slowly and carefully through the bushes.

"Robinson Crusoe," the voice called.

I followed the sound to a thick hedge.

"Crusoe," it called again.

"What does this voice want of me?" I asked.

I crept forward on all four paws. Then, suddenly, I saw the bushes rustling, and there was my Poll.

"Poll, come to me and you will be safe from whomever is calling to me." I motioned to the bird. "Quickly, I'll save you."

"Poor Robinson Crusoe!" he cried.

I stared at him, stunned and amazed.

"Robinson!" he cried.

"It's you—*you* were the one who was speaking!" I cried happily. "It just goes to show that you *can* teach an old parrot new tricks."

"Poor Robinson," Poll called.

"Oh, not necessarily," I said. "Let's try to be positive—and grateful." I was so happy that I wept.

It was the first time I had heard another voice in nearly twelve years.

Although Poll could talk, he wasn't exactly the best conversationalist in the world. So I did the best I could to be company for myself. I could talk to myself for hours, but there was no surprise in it, as I always knew what I was going to say back to myself. In the end, I sometimes felt lonelier than before. What good were all the creature comforts of home, when I was yearning for all the good things only a companion could bring—a pat on the head, a scratch behind the ears, or even a bath?

I began to notice more and more cats on the island. As they got used to me, they grew bolder and showed themselves more often. There were nearly twenty of them. They weren't great company, either.

"Must you purr so loudly?" I cried, as they often kept me awake at night.

Their sly way of walking bothered me, as did their indifference to the things I held dear—like games of fetch or chasing my tail. And their food was decidedly fishy.

"Two's company, but this is truly ridiculous," I said. I didn't want to be outnumbered. "This is quite a cat-astrophe!" I decided. "Shoo, I say! Go away! Then, whenever I heard a noise, I cried out, "Friend, foe—or feline?"

Time passed. I kept track of the seasons by the way my coat shed and thickened. Before I knew it, I had been on the island by myself for twenty years. I missed everything, but what was frightening was how hazy my memory of London and my life there was growing. I could remember having wonderful meals I had had in London, but I could no longer remember exactly what they had been. I could remember wearing fine clothes, but the colors and fabrics were hazy in my mind.

The one part of my former life in London that I still remembered clearly was my parents. I longed to get back to them. Every few months, I stood by the sea and watched for passing ships. I had firewood ready to build a great fire to draw attention to me, but every time I looked out to sea all I saw were the waves. The only thing I thought about was escape.

"I need someone to talk to," I said. I never got used to being alone. I always thought someone might rescue me.

One day, I was walking on the beach. I was thinking how lonely I felt, how I wished more than anything to see another human soul. Suddenly I came upon a footprint in the sand. Everything seemed to have stopped cold. I felt the fur stand up straight on the back of my neck. I looked around wildly, but even my keen eyes, which could spy a piece of kibble from thirty feet away, could see nothing. *It's only a mirage,* I thought. *I'm tired and I am seeing things.* I shut my eyes tightly and then opened them again. I expected the footprint to be gone. But there it was.

"How did a footprint get here?" I cried. "And whose footprint is it?" I stepped inside the print. It was four times bigger than my own. In fact, all four of my

paws might fit into the one print. I was so terrified that all my fur stood on end. My heart thundered in my ears. "Who knows what this person wants?" I said.

I went back to my house and buried my head under my front paws.

"Wait a minute, here," I said. "Why should I lie here and roll over and play dead for days? I should go out and tend to my corn, or milk one of the goats, or take a walk and get some exercise—do *something*." Although I kept nudging myself to do something, I couldn't leave my house—not that day, and not for days after, either.

"Scaredy cat! Scaredy cat!" called Poll.

"I don't see you going exploring," I told the bird. "You're a bird who may be part chicken yourself." But gradually, I began to feel ashamed by my lack of courage. Finally, carrying a musket in my mouth, I went outside to explore the situation.

I walked slowly, looking around, my heart pounding

so loudly that I was sure anyone else alive might hear it. I went back to the shoreline, but the ocean tides had washed the print away.

"Maybe I can tell myself it was just a dream," I said to myself. "Or maybe it was simply the print of my own foot. It's possible, right? I walk all over this island and don't pay much attention to where I am. That's what it must be. So what if it's bigger than my own foot? Maybe I've shrunk in size by now."

I had just about convinced myself and was ready to walk to the other side of the island, when suddenly I saw something in the distance.

Could it be? *It's not possible!* I thought. *I must be so hungry that I am imagining this feast! It must be a mirage!* My mouth began to water, for there, in front of me, the sand was spread with the ultimate delicacy! Bones! Lots and lots of bones!

"Bones!" I cried. "And me, with all this land to bury them in."

But whoever left this feast must be a sloppy house-keeper, I thought. *Doesn't he clean up after himself?* I moved closer and then saw something to make my fur stiffen and my whiskers wilt. To my great horror, I saw that these were not regular bones—they were the remains of people!

"Cannibals!" I cried. "There must be cannibals on the island." I was seized with a cold grip of terror. I was frozen in place, shivering with fear. My eyes locked on the bones. In the center of all the bones was a place where a great fire had been made. There was also a circle dug into the earth, where I supposed the cannibals had sat down to their horrible feasting.

What if they are still here—and still hungry? I thought. *I may be cute and cuddly, but what if they think I may also be . . . well . . .* delicious?

Boy, when Crusoe told his father that he had a real appetite for adventure, I don't think he meant this. It's a jungle out there, all right. Imagine! More than twenty years on an island, and the first people Crusoe might see are cannibals! . . . Speaking of jungles, let's wag on over to the urban jungle to see how Joe and I are doing in the park.

Chapter Twelve

It was six-thirty. . . . Bruno, the big neighborhood Doberman, growled and bounded toward Joe and Wishbone.

"He looks as if he's not in such a good mood," Wishbone said. "And we've got nothing to cool him down with. This calls for some special strategy, Joe. Command him to stop. He'll listen to you."

"Stop! Go home!" Joe shouted, as if he had heard Wishbone. Still, Bruno kept coming toward them.

"It didn't work," Wishbone said. "What's plan B? Come on, Joe, plan B. It comes after plan A. Don't we have a plan B?"

Joe was frozen in place, staring at the menacing Doberman.

Wishbone geared himself up. "Okay now, no need to be scared. Just because last time he made me turn tail and run is no reason to think he can do it again. Times have changed. I'm older now, wiser, stronger. Right? I have to rescue Joe," Wishbone said.

He drew himself up to his full height.

"Watch this diversionary tactic," Wishbone said. He raced around Bruno. "Hey, Bruno!" he yelped. "Pick on someone of your own species."

Wishbone yipped at Bruno's fur, drawing Bruno away from Joe.

"You're free, Joe," Wishbone called, just as Bruno snapped at his tail. "Hey! I need that tail," Wishbone said. "And wait, wait, stay away from my legs—I need them, too."

Joe snapped to attention. "Leave him alone, you big bully!" Joe commanded.

He bent down and grabbed up some loose dirt and threw it at Bruno, who growled and lunged forward, his teeth flashing.

"Uh-oh, not only didn't that work, but it seems as if the dog's even angrier than before," Joe said.

Joe looked around, then grabbed the flashlight from the bike and waved it menacingly at Bruno.

"Go home!" Joe ordered.

But Bruno barked extra loudly and came even closer, startling Joe so much that he dropped the flashlight, which rolled off into the darkness.

Joe waved his empty hands. "What am I going to do?" Joe cried. Desperate, he took Wanda's camera from his shoulder and was about to throw that at Bruno when suddenly he had an idea. "Brilliant!" he said. "Hey, Bruno!" Joe shouted. "Say 'cheese'!"

He snapped the camera shutter just as Bruno was about to clamp down on Wishbone's tail. The flash sizzled and a burst of light erupted, scaring Bruno, who yelped in great surprise and turned tail, running off in the distance.

"'Bye, now! Don't call us, we'll call you!" Wishbone said.

"Say 'double cheese'!" Joe said, snapping another flash picture.

Bruno whimpered and ran faster.

"Guess he doesn't want to wait for the prints to be developed," Wishbone said.

Joe bent down and rubbed Wishbone's fur. "Are you all right?"

"Sure, I am," Wishbone said. "I just *pretended* to be a little scared to throw Bruno off guard."

"Let's get going," Joe said.

They were coming to the end of Jackson Park. The trees thinned out and the park was getting a bit brighter.

"I can ride my bike now, I bet," Joe said. "And I can see the face of my watch now." He stopped. "A quarter to seven! But if I pedal fast, we should make it." He got on and pedaled, gliding along the path. "Oh, this feels much better. I didn't realize how tired I was," Joe said. "I'm going to put some speed into this."

"Is there room for the dog up there?" Wishbone asked hopefully.

Just then there was a loud *hiss*. The bike suddenly bucked forward, nearly throwing Joe to the ground. "Ow!" Joe cried. He sat up, feeling the tire. "Punctured!" he said. "I can't ride on it now."

"I guess that answers the question about catching a lift," Wishbone said.

"I talk the talk, so now I have to walk the walk," Joe said. He pushed his bike forward. "Let's go, Wishbone." He started walking forward and then stopped, breathing heavily. "I am so exhausted, and we have so little time. How are we ever going to make the game?" Joe said.

Can Joe and I make it to the game on time? Well, we'll certainly score points for trying! And speaking of trying, Crusoe's just about to find himself in one of his most dangerous situations yet!

Chapter Thirteen

Suddenly, I was surprised to see a light far from shore. A canoe was floating on the water, carrying many men. I had not seen men in more than twenty years, and I began to cry. It seemed such a strange and wondrous sight to me that I thought I must be dreaming. I kept looking at them to make sure that they were really men. "Yes, they have heads and feet and hands!" I said.

But then I began to worry. Were these the cannibals, or was this a rescue? I squinted. The men had long black hair that hung loose down their backs. Suddenly, I saw something that made the fur tighten on my back. The men were wearing necklaces made of small bones. Some of them even had bones worn like earrings or nose rings. *That can't be much fun when they sneeze*, I thought. The men certainly looked like savages to me. I quickly hid behind a tree.

The canoe came closer and closer, finally landing onshore. I saw ten men get out and start to examine the bones with enthusiasm. These really were the cannibals. Next, they dragged two men from the canoe and started to tie them up. One was frozen in place. The other one, a tall fellow in his middle twenties, began to untie the ropes that were around him and ran directly toward me! These prisoners must be the cannibals' lunch—or dinner! I knew that I must save the young man.

I began to motion to the savage with one of my front paws, making signs for him to come to me. "Follow me! There's a creek where we can swim to safety!"

He saw me and started running just as I did. Running for our lives, we reached the creek and didn't look back.

It was lucky for us that the cannibals couldn't swim. I dog-paddled furiously across the strong tide. When we got to the other shore, we were both panting and shivering, but safe. The cannibals and their canoe were nowhere to be seen.

"They must have gone back where they came from. We're safe for now," I said.

I took the savage to my house and showed him all around my place.

"I've got a warm bed, a table, a chair, food—and company," I said, pointing out Poll, who was sitting on top of the table. "Speaking of creature features, how about some food?" I asked. "Boy, action really activates my appetite."

I pulled out some raisins that I had dried in the broiling sun and offered them to the savage.

"Do you have a name?" I asked.

The savage blinked at me.

"Crusoe," I said, raising a paw. "I am Robinson Crusoe."

The savage was silent.

"Well, I shall call you Friday, since that is today by my calendar," I said. "Is that all right?"

Friday nodded.

Friday! That might seem like a funny name to you, but it worked its way into our language with the term "Gal Friday," which means a kind of do-it-all cheerful helper. However, instead of working on an island, it usually means working in an office! Me, I'm not just Joe's Dog Friday. I'm his Dog Monday, Tuesday—every dog day!

Friday! For some, it's the best day of the week. I knew Friday was a savage. I was not quite sure how we would get along, though I had hopes he might be company for me. His eyes sparkled. He seemed intelligent. He spoke a few words to me, but I could not understand them.

"I'll teach you English!" I said enthusiastically.

We studied each other.

I started off with simple words, like *yes* and *no, tree* and *food.* I repeated them over and over, pointing to the objects so he would understand.

"Tree," Friday said, pointing to an oak. "Yes," he said, when I offered him some raisins. "Food very good," he said.

Friday was a quick learner. We practiced every day.

In a few months, Friday and I were able to have real conversations.

"I've dreamed of this for years," I told him. "Now I actually have company!"

"You save Friday's life," he said.

I felt instantly touched.

I thought I might educate Friday, teaching him to read and write a little. We walked down to the damp sand by the water. I took up a stick in my mouth, drawing alphabet letters in the sand.

One of the island cats sauntered by and I pointed to it. "There," I said. "Cat. C-A-T." I drew the letters in the sand, spelling them out as I made them.

"Cat," said Friday.

D-O-G, I wrote. Then I said the word. "Dog—a wonderful and good creature."

"Dog," said Friday. "Man's best friend."

I taught Friday everything I could. I taught him how to plant, how to gather the crops, and how to read and write.

We passed five years this way. "I have been on this island twenty-five years now," I told Friday. "I need to get off, but I can't make a boat that will float."

"Friday show you," he said.

"Show me what?"

"Friday show you which tree to cut," he said. "My native island much like this one. With many same trees."

I followed Friday deep into the island's interior, where we came upon a grove of trees. He pointed to one. He knocked at it.

"Good wood," he said. "Good for boat."

It was my turn to be the student. I felt as if I were back at obedience school again. I watched Friday cut down the tree, helping him when he asked me. Then I sat back on my haunches, my tail wagging, and watched him start to carve out the inside of the tree. He wouldn't let me help.

"Watch," he said.

And so I did, until I recognized the shape of a canoe.

"This is wonderful!" I said. "How did you know how to do this?"

Friday smiled. "Friday just know," he said. After a while, he let me help. I followed his instructions with growing respect for the man.

I couldn't wait for each day to begin to find out what else I could learn from Friday. *If we get off this island, it will be because of him,* I thought.

After six months, we had a beautiful canoe. The only task that was left was for the two of us to push it toward the sea.

"Take rest now," Friday said. "We push canoe later."

A few days later, I came upon Friday sitting on the beach, staring out to sea. His face looked so unhappy that I thought something bad had happened to him. "What is it?" I asked, my tail wagging in encouragement.

Friday shook his head. "Friday misses his people," he said.

"I miss mine, too," I said.

"Friday wants to go home."

"We have a canoe now," I said. "We can take you home to your island. Then, if a large ship comes, I can go on to England."

I felt a quick, deep pain in my heart. I knew suddenly that I didn't want Friday to go home.

"Friday not want to go home without Crusoe," Friday said.

"Crusoe doesn't want you to go home without him," I said.

Friday's face lit up with his smile. I felt warm all over with happiness, from my nose to my wagging tail.

"Don't worry," I said. "I swear by my whiskers, we will leave this island together."

Friday and I had much to teach each other. Friday had built our canoe. He also showed me how we could catch fish from the ocean, using spears made out of sharpened wood. I, in turn, showed Friday how to make himself clothing from goatskin.

Once, I had thought Friday was only a savage who might be company for me. Now, I knew he was a true and good friend.

We worked and worked to pull the canoe out to sea. Friday got behind it and pushed with all his might, while I was at the front and pulled at it. We made little headway.

"At this rate, we won't get the canoe to the ocean until my fur has turned gray," I said. "Every time I turn around, another year has passed. It's been almost twenty-six years already since I was shipwrecked."

We stopped to rest. Then Friday helped me plant more corn. In the evening, we went to the sea to swim. Friday looked out to sea, squinting. He began to panic and leaped to his feet, pointing excitedly out over the ocean. I stood up and then I saw, too—the six canoes headed our way.

"Company's coming again," I said. "Until I know who is in those boats, I think I want to hold off being the welcome wagon."

Friday stared at the ocean again. I trained my eyes and then I saw just who was on the boats. "Bone necklaces. Bone earrings. It's those same cannibals. And this time there are twenty-one of them."

"That be twenty-one too many," said Friday.

Chapter Fourteen

I paced the sand, waving my tail back and forth to calm myself. "We're outnumbered, which is not a good position to be in with cannibals," I said. "I like a bone as much as anyone else, but this isn't what I had in mind."

"What we do?" Friday asked.

"We have to fight them," I said. "Do you think you can shoot a musket?"

Friday hesitated for a moment. "If it not shoot me first," he finally decided.

I gave Friday a musket and showed him how to use it. He was a quick learner. I had no fear that Friday would not be a great help to me.

We carefully entered the woods, from where we watched the savages land on the beach. "They have prisoners again," Friday said, and he gasped. "Look!"

We watched the savages tie up a man and then push him roughly into a canoe close to shore.

"Friday, you must do exactly what I command you to do," I said. "When I give the signal, we fire upon them. Okay?"

"Okay," Friday said.

We ran back to the house and got more of the ammunition that I had taken from the ship. By the time we got back to the beach, the cannibals had made a fire and were sitting around it.

"Do you understand what they're saying?" I asked Friday.

Friday nodded. "They going to eat prisoner. Friday and Crusoe must stop them," Friday said.

I looked at Friday, thinking what a good man he was, and how lucky for me that he understood the cannibals' language.

We sneaked up on the cannibals by hiding behind some tall trees. My heart was pounding with fright because, even with the muskets, we were still seriously outnumbered. Every single step we took seemed so loud that I was sure the cannibals were going to hear us and then finally see us.

We ran from tree to tree, keeping out of sight.

"Ready?" I whispered to Friday.

"Friday ready," he said, taking careful aim.

"Fire!" I shouted, and we both did. My shot whizzed past them, missing, but Friday clipped one of the cannibals in the leg, wounding him.

Instantly the cannibals leaped up. They were shouting and screaming. They began to run back toward their canoes, all the while looking wildly behind them. Two of the cannibals began to drag their wounded companion with them.

"What are they saying?" I asked Friday.

"They say this be punishment from their gods." Friday frowned and strained to hear what else the

cannibals were saying. I perked up both my ears, too, as if I might suddenly understand the language.

"Quick! While they are running, let's try to free the prisoner!" I cried. "You fire, and I'll rush forward and try to get him out."

I was so terrified that every bit of fur I had was standing straight on end. Friday suddenly fired, making the cannibals scream in terror even more, and that was my cue. I ran out among them, as fast as my paws could carry me. Two of the cannibals stared at me in amazement, and then, to my horror, in hunger. I took up my gun and tried to fire, but I found that the weapon suddenly jammed and wouldn't shoot.

"Help, Friday, help!" I shouted. "Friday, fire!"

Friday fired again, scattering the cannibals away from me. They looked back at me one more time. Luckily, Friday fired at them again. This time, they ran toward the sea and their canoe.

I rushed to the man who was tied up onshore. I nudged him with my nose, which was damp and cool. I thought my touch might revive him.

The savages were terrified and began screaming. Some of them suddenly found the canoe Friday had built and began pushing it into the sea, along with their own canoe.

"They say they leave island and will never return," Friday told me.

"Wait!" I yelped to the cannibals. "That is *our* canoe, not yours."

The savages climbed into the canoes, and they paddled farther and farther out into the ocean. Friday and I had managed to chase them off the island in no time at all.

"They not come back," Friday said. "But it make Friday not want to go to nearby islands."

"They took our canoe anyway," I said.

There was one last man onshore, bound hand and foot, and looking half dead. "To the rescue," I said. I took some rope up in my teeth, pulled on it, and untied the poor wretch's hands and feet. The weary man groaned and tried to sit up.

Just then, Friday came over.

"Friday, help me, would you, please?" I asked. "This man is so weak that he can hardly walk. Speak to him, tell him we've saved him, and maybe give him a drink from the bottle you always carry."

I sat back on my haunches, exhausted. Nothing prepared me for the look of shock on Friday's face when he gazed down at the man. His eyes sparkled. It would have moved anyone to tears to have seen how Friday kissed him, embraced him, cried, laughed, hallooed, jumped about, danced, and sang.

"What is it?" I asked. "Do you know this man?"

By this time Friday and the man were weeping and laughing all at the same time. "Know him?" said Friday. "He my father!"

I had never been so moved in my life. Friday would not leave his father's side for a moment. He rubbed his father's hands and feet and kissed them, and he sang to his father and professed his love and devotion for him. There didn't seem to be enough Friday could do for his beloved father. Friday went all the way back to the house he shared with me to get food and water, and he fed his father himself.

"I thought I never see you again," Friday said to his father.

Seeing Friday's kindness and devotion to his father made me like and respect him even more. But it also made me like and respect myself a little less. I began to think about my own father, and about how carelessly I had left him. I wept, covering my eyes with my paws. I wished with all my heart that I could see my father, and he could see for himself how I had changed. I had run off for adventures almost twenty-six years ago. I had now become the kind of man I knew he would be proud of. I would give my right front paw if he could only see how I had matured.

Chapter Fifteen

Joe and Wishbone walked block after block. It was a funny thing, Wishbone thought. Even though each of the blocks was the exact same length, every one they traveled seemed longer and harder to walk.

"I can't get tired now," Joe said.

Then it started to drizzle.

"Great," Joe said. "Just what we need." Joe glanced at his watch again. "It's five to seven. We have five minutes!"

"Good thing I took all those dog aerobics," Wishbone said, panting. He stepped up his pace a bit. "I know I wanted to walk, but I meant *walk*—not *run*."

After a while, though, Joe began to slow down. "Boy, this is more tiring than I thought it would be," he said.

Wishbone frisked around Joe. "Come on, Joe, you can do it! I know you can! Think of it as a challenge! We're almost there! There's nothing we can't do when we put our minds—not to mention all six of our legs—to the task!"

Joe checked his watch again and then peered into

the distance. "Is it my imagination, or is the town getting lighter?" He turned back to look toward where they had come from. "It's still dark back there."

"Oh, I can see the color of my own fur now," Wishbone said. "And I can see some buildings up ahead."

"Look!" Joe said excitedly. There's a light in the distance. It's the school, and it's all lit up. And look. Over there. There's another light—and another. The blackout didn't affect this part of town. We made it, Wishbone." He stumbled, then righted himself. "But I'm so tired, I can hardly stand."

Joe and Wishbone hurried inside the school. There were big signs posted, pointing toward the gym. "Let's go," Joe said, rushing.

Joe and Wishbone ran down the corridors, arriving at the gym in what seemed like just seconds. The stands were only half-filled, and the players milled about on the sidelines.

"I just have to get enough strength to play," Joe said.

"What, no cheerleaders?" Wishbone said. "Never

mind. I'll play that part. And don't forget, Joe, this dog is up for action—I could play, too!"

"Sit in the stands," Joe told Wishbone.

Joe looked around. There were lots of empty seats. None of the people from his neighborhood was even there. He scanned the crowd.

"David's not here," he said. "Neither is Sam. And there are only a few of the students from my school."

Joe slid along a wall.

"I don't know how I can play when I'm feeling so exhausted," Joe said wearily.

Just then, Ronny, one of Joe's teammates, came over to him. "Joe, I'm so glad you're here. This is so weird, man. Some parts of town weren't affected by the blackout at all, and the kids who live there had no problem getting here. I almost didn't get here myself, but my sister drove me. We picked up some of the other kids along the way."

"Why didn't you pick me up?" Joe asked.

"We went by your house, but you had left already," he said.

"Oh, I left early," Joe said.

"It took us forever, anyway, because of the traffic."

"It took us forever, too," Joe said.

Joe looked around. Suddenly, he straightened. Over by the wall was the eighth-grade coach. He was a big man in a striped shirt and a blue baseball cap.

"The coach is writing something down on a notepad," Joe said. "I bet it's the names of players he thinks have talent. All I kept thinking originally was how I could get him to notice me, but now all I'm thinking is how can I get him *not* to."

Wishbone barked encouragement.

"Shh!" Joe hushed him. "You don't want to get kicked out."

Joe tried to look like a champion.

"I've got to go change," Joe said. "I'm lucky that I wore my gym shorts under my pants."

Joe left to go change in the locker room.

Wishbone climbed up the stands, winding his way past the people sitting there. "Excuse me, excuse me, dog coming through." He wedged onto a bench. "Ah, now I can see."

Joe ran out onto the court, joining the other members of his team. They smiled and clapped him on the back. "Thank goodness you got here," one of Joe's fellow teammates said.

"He looks tired," Wishbone said. "And the other team looks . . . tall."

Joe's game plan—to help his team—might not work out as he hoped. Speaking of great teamwork, let's see how Crusoe and Friday are doing.

Chapter Sixteen

Time passed even more quickly with the good company of Friday. Before I knew it, I had been on the island for more than twenty-eight years. *That's longer than I lived in England,* I thought. We didn't build another canoe to venture out to the other islands because we knew cannibals lived there. Although they had not come back to our island, we didn't want to go to theirs.

One day, I was sleeping, paws over my face, when Friday awoke me with his calls. "Crusoe! They come! They come!"

I jumped up. "Who?"

Friday shook his head. His father said something, and Friday told me what it was. "He say a tall ship come," Friday explained. Friday then pointed, and I saw a tall ship with a huge, rounded sail. It seemed to be approaching the island.

Suddenly, I was worried. Friday and I and his father did not know whether these people were friends or enemies, and my built-in radar for such matters seemed to have shut down.

116

We watched, and lo and behold, there were men who looked like Englishmen coming ashore from the main ship in small boats.

"Land at last," one said.

"They speak English, they look English—they *must* be English," I said. I took a deep sniff. "They even smell English."

I was happy until I saw some of the sailors prodding three others fiercely with their muskets.

"What is this?" I cried.

I watched as three seamen were tied up with their hands behind their backs. They were roughly forced on the shore and flung down on the sand, where they couldn't move.

"We'll be back, and when we are, it won't be pretty," one of the men called to the prisoners.

The other men left, moving deep into the forest.

"They mean to kill the prisoners," I said.

"Then they kill us, too, if they see us," Friday whispered.

"We can't let that happen," I said.

We were terrified. We could have gone back to the house and hidden. Or we could have fled to the far side of the island, where we would probably not be found. But the moaning of the prisoners kept us pinned in place.

"We must help men," Friday said.

"Wait—" I said. We waited until we heard and saw no signs of the other men, for we did not want to be ambushed.

Then we carefully approached the prisoners. When they looked up and saw us, they gasped in fear.

"Gentlemen, do not be frightened by me," I whispered. "Perhaps you have a friend near you when you did not expect it. Loyal. Trustworthy."

The men continued to stare at us, some of them with tears running down their faces.

"What has happened here?" I asked, bending down and cutting their ropes with my teeth.

"I was the commander of that ship," one of the men told me. "My men have mutinied against me. They'll be back to kill us."

"Where are your enemies?" I asked.

"In the forest," he answered, pointing. "Two of the men are brutal. They would have killed me right on the ship and flung me into the sea if the rest had agreed to it. That's why I think those others will come to their senses and return to my command."

"I can help you," I told the captain. "But if I do, I want you to promise two things: one, that you will not exert any power while on this island; and, two, you must give me and my companion, Friday, and his father free passage on your ship back to England."

"Done!" he cried. "Plus, if you help me, I will owe my life to you."

I gave him a musket and bit the ropes from the other two men. Then we all ventured deeper into the island's interior. The mutineers were all sitting in a field, drinking and laughing. Their muskets were at their sides. Unless we caught them by surprise, they could easily leap up, grab their weapons, and kill us all almost instantly.

We hid in the forest. "Ready—" I whispered.

I kept my ears back and my tail low. Friday and his father crouched behind me. The captain and his men aimed their muskets, ready to fire.

"Aim—" I whispered. "But keep yourself under cover."

The mutineers toasted one another. I felt my heart pounding in fear.

"Fire!" I shouted.

We shot into the air, startling the mutineers so that they leaped up.

"We surprise them!" Friday shouted. He was fearless. While the rest of us were still hidden by the woods, he ran straight into them. One of the mutineers reached for his musket.

"Friday! Watch out!" I yelped.

I couldn't wait for Friday to react. I had to save him. I ran from the wooded area right toward the mutineers. Reaching the mutineer who was about to grab his musket, I quickly kicked his weapon away from him with my paws.

"Don't move!" I cried, pointing my own musket at the gang of mutineers.

"Or what?" said a voice.

Suddenly, I felt a musket pressed up against my neck.

"Don't shoot Crusoe," Friday called. He threw down his musket. "Friday do anything to save life of Crusoe."

The mutineer who held the musket against the scruff of my neck laughed.

"And I will do anything to save my ship," said the captain, coming into view. He pointed his musket at the very man who held a weapon on me. "Drop it," the captain told him, "or I will shoot you."

"It's the captain!" the mutineers cried.

"If you do not surrender, you will be taken back to England and be hanged," the captain said. "Surrender, and I will show you mercy."

Slowly, one by one, the mutineers held their hands up in the air.

"How could you do this?" the captain shouted.

The mutineers were silent.

"It was a mistake," one of them finally called out. "We were forced into it."

I kept the musket on them as the captain spoke.

"I will spare your lives if you give me your word that you are sorry and that you will help us get back the ship and set sail for England."

"We are sorry! We will help you return home!" the men cried.

"Twenty-six mutineers are still aboard my ship," said the captain. "They'll shortly be wondering what happened to the rest of their crewmen who came ashore. They will be coming onshore themselves to investigate. We will be outnumbered, for sure."

"We need to divide and conquer," I said. I was deeply afraid the ship would leave and we would be stranded, but I had an idea. "Captain, we could travel farther down the island and yell 'hello' to the ship. The men on board will think we are mutineers, and some of them will come ashore. When they do, we can over-power them. We can keep doing the exact same thing until there are almost no men left on board. Then we can seize the ship ourselves."

"You must be very careful," the captain said. "Those men are murderers. They'd just as soon kill you as look upon you. This task won't be easy."

We carefully made our way farther down the shoreline, where there were lots of trees closer to the beachfront. We hid behind the trees so the men on board the ship couldn't see us. Friday and the captain called out to the ship. As sure as I have fur, some of the men from the ship responded and then came ashore.

"Where are you?" they called, looking around the bare shoreline.

"Come closer," Friday replied, luring them into the woods.

"Will they take the bait?" I whispered.

"Come here quick," Friday called again.

The mutineers came closer and closer to us, their muskets at their sides. This was just the chance I was sniffing for. We waited until they were so close to our hiding place that I could have reached out one paw and touched them.

"*Now!*" I shouted.

Then we pounced forward and fired our muskets, surprising the men so much that they didn't have time to lift up their own weapons.

"You are our prisoners," I said. "Now you must call to the ship and tell others to come ashore."

Other sailors came ashore, in groups of four, until we had overcome almost all but four men who were still on board. The captain stood guard over the prisoners, his musket aimed at their heads. "Don't you dare move," he ordered.

The ship had come in closer with each batch of men that had landed. It was now close enough for us to try to seize it.

"There may be only four men left on board, but remember how dangerous they are," the captain warned.

We waited until night, when the sky was so dark that it was impossible to see where the water reached the shore. Friday and I left the captain and Friday's father to guard the prisoners. I must say, Friday and I were as quiet as cats as we approached the water, our muskets held alert and ready.

Quietly, we pushed a canoe back into the water and floated toward the ship. The night was eerie and still and full of danger. I could hear myself breathing, my tongue hanging out as I panted. Any moment, I feared that the men on board might wake up and then fire on us.

We finally got to the ship. "This is it," I whispered to Friday. I clasped his hand in my two front paws. "If anything happens to me or to you, I just want you to know how brave I think you are. I want you to know I love you as my friend."

Friday squeezed my paws. "Friday love Crusoe, too," he whispered.

There was a long rope ladder hanging from the ship. We climbed it carefully. I held my musket in my mouth.

I pulled myself up on deck, waiting for Friday. I suddenly turned, only to find a musket pointed right at my nose. . . .

Chapter Seventeen

I saw my life pass before my eyes. I thought of my father, who I would not have a chance to say good-bye to. I thought of never seeing England again. Suddenly, though, Friday pulled up on deck and fired, wounding the sailor in the leg so that he fell.

The other three men suddenly raced up on deck, waving their muskets and then shooting at us.

"Surrender, or you are all lost!" they cried out.

Friday and I didn't listen. Head down, I whisked between the legs of one of the sailors, so that he tumbled onto the deck, then fell into the sea. There were only two more sailors to overcome. One of the sailors had his musket pointed right at me.

"Give up," he ordered.

"Never," I barked. I bared my teeth, growling deep in my throat. Then I leaped up at the weapon pointed right at me. We wrestled, both of us falling onto the deck, until I managed to get the musket away from him. I held it in my mouth and pointed it at him.

"Stop!" cried the other sailor. He turned his attention—and his musket—away from Friday for one fatal second. It was long enough for Friday to leap behind the sailor and knock the weapon from his hand, kicking it high into the air. The musket splashed into the sea, and Friday grabbed the sailor.

I was so excited I could barely speak. "We have taken you both as prisoners," I said. "The rest of your mutinous crew is held onshore."

"We surrender," said the sailors. "The ship is yours."

We took the two sailors back to shore in the canoe. We brought them to the other mutineers. As soon as they saw their captain, they wept. "Please don't kill us," they begged.

The captain shook his head. "You are all prisoners and will go back to England and stand trial," he said.

He tied them up. The men were put in canoes and taken to board the ship. The captain had other men stand guard over them.

The captain turned to me, smiling. "Now I will keep my promise. I will take you, your man Friday, and his father back to England—or wherever it is that you want to go."

"England, it is," I said with glee. "Though Spain sounds nice, too."

I could not believe that I was really going to leave my island.

"It's true, right?" I kept asking the captain.

"Absolutely," he insisted.

Before we left, I took the captain on a tour of my

island. I showed him my house and my favorite digging spots and all of the places where I liked to roll in the mud. He greatly admired everything that I had done and exclaimed over and over again about how wonderfully resourceful I had been.

Leaving was harder than I thought. "Will you and your father come to England with me?" I asked Friday. "I think I would miss you too much if you didn't."

Friday smiled. "Friday and father gladly come with you."

"Great," I barked in delight. "Let's gather up what treasures we can carry. Everyone in England will be amazed."

Friday did not take much, but I carried with me my goatskin clothing, my umbrella, and my parrot. I also took, with great humor, the money I had collected when I first had become a castaway. Now the gold might be of use to me once I was back in England. I dreamed of the bones it might buy me.

Thus, I left my island in December, during the late 1680s. I had been on the island twenty-eight years, two months, and nineteen days.

Never was I happier to climb aboard a ship. "I will have my sea legs back in no time—all four of them," I said. The very thought set my tail wagging.

The whole trip back, I kept thinking about England. I watched Friday with his father, the two of them loving and affectionate, and I ached to see my own parents. *Now they will be proud of me,* I thought. *Now I want nothing more than what they wanted for me—to settle down and stay in one place.*

The voyage home took a very long time—more

than one year, in fact. We arrived back in England on the 11th of June, 1688.

As soon as we arrived, I rushed from the dock to find my parents. "Wait until you meet them," I told Friday.

But when I got to my home and knocked on the door, a stranger answered.

"I'm looking for the Crusoes," I said politely.

The stranger shook his head. "They haven't lived here in ten years," he said. "They both died."

Died! I sat down on the curb and wept so hard I made my fur damp. I could not stop crying until I felt a hand on my head.

"Do not feel bad," Friday said. "What is important is you return now to your parents. You now live life the way they would want Crusoe to. That is way to honor their memory."

I dried my teary eyes with the tip of my tail. "Friday, you are right," I said.

I bought a house in London with the gold from the wrecked ship. It was a home that was big enough to share with Friday and his beloved father. We were all happy and content.

After a while I fell in love with a young school-teacher named Helen. She had golden curly hair and a sweet smile. We married and bought another house, close to Friday and his father, who always came for Sunday dinner. My wife and I had two children: a girl, Ruthie; and a boy, Douglas. Both of my children loved to hear me tell the tale of my adventures on the island. My wife urged me to write down the stories. "People could learn from you," she said.

And so I did. When I was finished writing my tale, the only thing left for me to do was to publish my journal. I knew that Helen was right. Others could benefit from my experience.

So, all's well that ends well with Crusoe. But Joe's big game is just beginning.

Chapter Eighteen

The game began. All the players gathered in the center of the court for a center jump ball. Wishbone wagged his whole body in encouragement. "Take your time, Joe, take your time," he called.

The referee tossed the ball into the air above the centers. The center on Joe's team tapped it toward Joe, who leaped into the air and grabbed it.

"Contact has been made," Wishbone yelped.

Joe ran to the basket, dodging the other team's guard, but just as he neared the basket, he stumbled and nearly fell.

"Joe," Wishbone called.

Joe was staring at the eighth-grade coach, who was carrying a clipboard and writing something down. At that moment, the other team's guard knocked the ball from Joe's hands.

"Oh, no!" Joe exclaimed.

"It's okay, Joe. You've got another chance," Wishbone called. "It's like when I chase cars. Another one always comes along."

Joe quickly leaped for the ball again, missing. The

game continued. The other team scored two baskets, and one foul shot, and then there was a ten-minute halftime. When the game started up again, Joe seemed doubly determined, from what Wishbone could see.

"You can do it, Joe," Wishbone called.

Sure enough, it wasn't long before Joe grabbed the ball again. This time, he seemed ready. He kept his eyes on the basket. He didn't once look over at the eighth-grade coach. He ran toward the basket, panting, so exhausted it made Wishbone yearn for his own dog bed just to watch Joe. When it came time for Joe to make a basket, Joe concentrated.

"Oh, he's got that look he gets when he's really serious about something," Wishbone said.

Joe crouched.

"And it's a—" Wishbone cried.

The ball sailed up toward the hoop in a perfect arc. Time seemed to move in slow motion. In that moment, the ball nudged the rim and then bounced back down.

"—a miss," Wishbone said with disappointment. "Oh, no. Joe. A miss."

The other team snapped up the ball, while Joe stood there, astonished. His team rushed past him. Then Joe went into action, moving in with them, trying to stop the ball.

The crowd cheered. A boy on Joe's team grabbed the ball and swung it cleanly into the hoop. Then a bell rang.

"They won!" Wishbone said. "Joe's team won." He edged his way down the stands. "Make way. Dog coming through."

The crowd was spilling on to the basketball floor, clapping Joe's team on the back. Wishbone edged up to the winning team, which was gathered around the coach.

"You all played really, really well," the coach said. "All of you should be proud of yourselves, because I know I am."

"Me, too, Joe," Wishbone said, rubbing against Joe's leg. He perked up his nose. "Wait, I smell something familiar. Let me just fine-tune things a bit here." He took another, deeper sniff. "Ellen's here, Joe. And . . . and Wanda. I wonder if she has some of those blackout sandwiches with her."

"Joe, hi. I'm sorry we got here so late," Ellen said, putting one arm around him. "Did you get my note? My car is still at the gas station. I took a taxi and looked all over for you so I could give you a ride to the game—if it was going to be played. I even stopped by Wanda's house and asked her for her help. She told me you had left quite a while ago. She didn't want to drive, so we grabbed another taxi and came here."

"The blackout really messed up my schedule," Joe said. "And there was this little girl who was lost. Wishbone and I spent a lot of time and effort to make sure we got her safely back to her home. Then Wishbone and I got attacked by a dog in the park—"

"A really *big* dog," Wishbone said.

"You did all that," Ellen said, "and you still made it here?"

"Spectacular!" said Wanda.

"I failed," Joe said glumly. "I did my best, but I was just too tired."

Ellen smiled. "I think you succeeded," she said. "And there will be lots of other chances, Joe."

"I played terribly."

"You did an incredibly brave thing," Ellen said. "You found your way across town in a blackout and made it to the game in time. You helped your team."

"And you fought battles along the way," Wanda said proudly.

"I let the team down."

"The team won," said Ellen. "And you didn't let anyone down—least of all yourself. You showed initiative and spunk and extreme bravery—not to mention loyalty."

"Loyalty. A boy with the soul of a dog is a beautiful thing," Wishbone said.

"I agree," Wanda said. "Joe, you're terrific."

Wishbone perched himself on his hind legs. "And what about the dog?" he coaxed. "Let's all take just a moment or two and praise the dog."

Ellen smiled. "Come on. Let's go home and celebrate. We can order pizza. I'll try to call another taxi."

"Celebrate?" Joe asked.

"That's right," Ellen said. "Celebrate."

They had to wait twenty minutes for a taxi. The whole time Joe told the story of how he had made it to the game. "Don't leave anything out," Wishbone said.

When the taxi arrived, Joe was telling more of his story. "You can continue telling us the tale in the taxi," Ellen said.

They were riding back home in the blackout, the streets still dark and scary-looking, when suddenly one of the office buildings lit up.

"Hey!" Joe said. "Does this mean what I think it does?"

Another building suddenly lit up. Then another.

Wishbone barked. "I can see. I can see. There's my favorite fire hydrant. Yoo-hoo! I'll be seeing you soon," he called.

"The blackout is finally ending," Ellen said. "What a relief."

There were so many lights on now, and Oakdale seemed so bright, that it was nearly blinding. Wishbone blinked. "I wish I had brought my sunglasses," he said.

"Now everything looks familiar," Joe said. "You can make out the houses and the cars and the lawns."

"You deserve a reward," Ellen said when they were inside their house. She held up one finger and then went into the kitchen.

The kitchen, Wishbone thought. *That's always a promising location.* "Oh, Ellen, need any help in there?"

Ellen came out carrying a carrot cake on a tray. Spelled out across the top of the frosting was an inscription that read: CHAMP.

"Champ? But I'm not a champ," Joe said, shaking his head.

Ellen ruffled his hair. "Oh, yes, you are, Joe. You're always a champ to me. What you did tonight proves it.

I ordered this cake at the bakery yesterday. Luckily, I left the house early enough today to pick it up before the blackout hit. When I first came home to see if you were here, I put it in the kitchen."

"Anything for me on that tray, Ellen, exalted keeper of the snacks, friend to dogs?" Wishbone said. He stood up on his hind legs. "I mean, look how cute I am when I'm begging."

"Oh, Wishbone, you can have some cake, too," Ellen said, and she gave him a slice of it.

Wishbone gobbled down the cake. "Carrot. Good for my eyes."

"I'm really proud of you, Joe," Ellen said.

"You are?"

Ellen nodded. "You didn't give up. You showed great resourcefulness, Joe."

"I've got something for you, too," Wanda said. She dug into her purse. "It's not really hot off the presses just yet—it's just a rough sketch I made during halftime. I thought you might like to see some mockup pages from tomorrow's *Chronicle*." Wanda waved a stack of papers.

She handed one to Joe.

"Wait. What about me?" Wishbone asked. "Can't we just forget that little incident in which I chewed up last week's news? I mean, those were big stories. I had to digest them."

Joe stared at the paper. "Look. There's a space for my picture, right on the front page." He looked at the article in amazement. It was titled: "Local Boy Refuses to Let Blackout Stop Him from Big Game." Joe grinned from ear to ear.

The Oakdale Chronicle

Local boy refuses to let blackout stop him from Big Game

"And that's not all," Wanda said, pointing to the front page. "There on the bottom are spaces for all the photographs you took, with your name underneath each one."

"I only took a few pictures," Joe admitted. "And they were of a really angry dog."

Wanda hesitated. "But that's wonderful," she said. "I can caption it something like: 'Even Mad Dog Doesn't Stop Boy from His Journey.'"

Joe smiled.

"You'll have your name under the photos you took. That's called a byline," Wanda said. "If that's not being famous, I don't know what is."

"A byline!" Joe marveled. "I never had a byline before."

"Read all about it!" Wanda proclaimed.

Joe's famous! Just like Robinson Crusoe, his adventure found its way into print so that others could read about it—and learn from it. It just goes to show you what you can do with a little initiative—and a great dog like me. Thinking big has always been my special talent—and that includes thinking big about some serious digging. So, 'bye for now . . . until the next tale wags along.

About Daniel Defoe

He was a convict, a soldier, a government spy, and he was also one of our greatest writers. That was Daniel Defoe.

No one knows exactly when Daniel Defoe was born. Some scholars think it was in 1660, but they know for sure he was born in London, England. Defoe started out his career as a businessman, but he took up writing when his business failed. He didn't write *Robinson Crusoe* until he was fifty-eight years old!

Defoe is remembered not just for being versatile, but also for his speed. He wrote essays and pamphlets as well as novels. And he could write a whole novel in just a few days.

Defoe was put in jail for writing a pamphlet that the English government and the Church didn't like. The government set him free on the condition that he would be a spy. He did so, but he was exposed as a spy after only a little while. What was he to do then? Why, write *Robinson Crusoe*.

Sadly, although *Robinson Crusoe* is considered to be one of the greatest works of literature ever written, Defoe died in near poverty.

About Robinson Crusoe

In 1666, The Great Fire of London raged through Daniel Defoe's neighborhood, stopping just one block short of his home. It was this incredible good fortune that made Defoe believe that some people could miraculously survive a disaster—just like his world-famous fictional character, Robinson Crusoe,

who survived a storm at sea that drowned everyone else on his ship.

Robinson Crusoe almost didn't get written. Daniel Defoe lived in a time when the novel, as we know it, didn't exist. To appeal to readers, a book had to be about some uplifting subject, like a Greek myth or a fable. Or it had to be a true account of some event. Made-up stories were considered to be lies, and good people avoided them!

Defoe wanted his work to be read, and he decided the best way for that to happen was to write *Robinson Crusoe* as if it had really occurred. He made his novel seem more true by basing his tale on an account of a real sailor, Alexander Selkirk, who had been cast away on a desert island for five years. Defoe also made his novel seem even more authentic by adding what is called a *preface*. A preface is an introduction or explanation. Defoe's made-up preface was supposedly written by Crusoe's editor, who claimed that the tale was all true.

The result? One of the most thrilling and beloved books of all time. Like Wishbone, any reader can be captivated by Crusoe's struggle for survival—without food, shelter, or supplies. *Robinson Crusoe* is a fascinating adventure story, a heartfelt moral tale, and a wonderful account of a special friendship. It could be the one novel *you* might want to take to a desert island with you.

About Caroline Leavitt

Daniel Defoe's *Robinson Crusoe* is one of Caroline Leavitt's favorite books—just as Wishbone is one of her favorite dogs! Writing about the two in this WISHBONE novel was certainly a great thrill.

An award-winning author, Caroline has written six novels, including another WISHBONE novelization, *The Prince and the Pooch,* based on Mark Twain's *The Prince and the Pauper.* Although her novels are written for adults, her last book, *Living Other Lives,* was named one of the best books of 1996 for teenagers by the New York City Public Library. She has also written magazine articles and screenplays for movies.

Although she loves the book *Robinson Crusoe,* Caroline doesn't think she'd like being marooned on a desert island. She prefers to be a castaway in her 124-year-old house with all the comforts of home—including her husband, Jeff; baby son, Max; and tortoise, Minnie. She'd be willing to add a dog to her household if it was as smart, cute, and talkative as Wishbone.

Now Playing on Your VCR...

Two exciting WISHBONE® stories on video!

Ready for an adventure? Then leap right in with **Wishbone**™ as he takes you on a thrilling journey through two great action-packed stories. First, there are haunted houses, buried treasure, and mysterious graves in two back-to-back episodes of *A Tail in Twain*, starring **Wishbone** as Tom Sawyer. Then, no one is more powerful than **Wishbone**, in *Hercules* Hercules...or rather *Unleashed*, featuring exciting new footage! It's more fun than a flea dip! It's **Wishbone** on home video.

WISHBONE™

Available wherever videos are sold.